"I've wanted to touch you all night," Gabe murmured

He unzipped Maggie's dress, easing the velvet garment from her shoulders. His fingers slipped under her hair and lower, to skim over her breasts and drop the velvet that barely covered them.

"Don't stop," she whispered. Maggie felt warm and languorous, sultry and inexperienced, shy and yet very aroused.

"Tell me what you like," he said, thumbing her nipples into tight peaks. His own arousal was building.

"This is a very good start," she managed to say, closing her eyes and leaning back against his bare chest.

Then he undressed her, slowly and with kisses. The silk garter belt and black stockings she'd found last summer in a box of old linens made Gabe draw in his breath. "I have a secret passion for vintage clothing," she confessed.

"A secret passion, hmm." Gabe leaned forward and, holding her hips, ran his tongue along the silk covered elastic. "I think," he said with a smile, "that Christmas has come a few days early...."

Dear Reader,

Merry Christmas! The MONTANA MATCHMAKERS have concluded the season with an attempt to find a new daddy for a little girl—and in time for Christmas, no less. But this particular little girl is determined that none other than Gabe O'Connor, a man her mother hasn't spoken to in four years, should be her stepfather. Because he can cook. Because his son is her best friend. And because she likes his truck better than her mother's.

And of course Louisa Bliss has found romance, too, much to her sister's consternation. All in all, the elderly Bliss sisters prove that it's never too late to find romance, especially in Montana.

I hope you enjoyed my miniseries. If there is someone you'd like The Hearts Club to find a match for, please let me—and Ella Bliss—know about it. We'll do our best!

Happy Reading,

Kristine Rolofson
P.O. Box 323
Peace Dale, RI 02883

Books by Kristine Rolofson

HARLEQUIN TEMPTATION
802—BLAME IT ON COWBOYS* Boots & Beauties 1
819—BLAME IT ON BABIES* Boots & Beauties 2
    BLAME IT ON TEXAS (Harlequin Single Title)*
    Boots & Beauties 3
842—A WIFE FOR OWEN CHASE* Montana Matchmakers 1
850—A BRIDE FOR CALDER BROWN* Montana Matchmakers 2

Kristine Rolofson
A MAN FOR MAGGIE MOORE

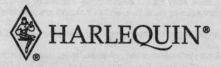

HARLEQUIN®

TORONTO • NEW YORK • LONDON
AMSTERDAM • PARIS • SYDNEY • HAMBURG
STOCKHOLM • ATHENS • TOKYO • MILAN • MADRID
PRAGUE • WARSAW • BUDAPEST • AUCKLAND

To my friend Kim,
who cheers me on with faxes, e-mails and chocolates
and who waits patiently for each book to be finished
so we can finally go out to dinner.

ISBN 0-373-25958-1

A MAN FOR MAGGIE MOORE

Copyright © 2001 by Kristine Rolofson.

This edition published by arrangement with Harlequin Books S.A.

Visit us at www.eHarlequin.com

Printed in U.S.A.

"I'VE HAD a special matchmaking request," Ella announced, setting her cards on the table in a neat pile. "And I think we should consider it."

"But the festival's over," Missy declared, as if the other three members of the Hearts Club weren't aware of the obvious. "And Christmas is only ten days away."

"We know, dear." Ella tried not to sigh. "And we've had a busy time of it, too. But I think we need to consider this one."

"Is it someone on the list?" Grace asked. Once a week the four elderly women gathered in the Bliss sisters' dining room and played cards, among other things, such as carrying on the town's tradition of successful matchmaking. They'd missed their usual Thursday afternoon meeting, due to Missy not feeling quite well and Grace needing to shop with her daughter, so they'd agreed to meet on Friday night instead.

And what a Friday night it was, Ella thought, remembering Robert's excited announcement.

"Yes, in a way." Ella, self-appointed leader of the group, was especially pleased with the past six weeks' accomplishments. Owen Chase was happy with his new wife, and Calder Brown's wedding—his second attempt to marry the lovely new baker—was tomorrow morning. The groom's grandfather had called an hour ago and invited them all to attend. Ella had even splurged on a new dress—supposed to be worn last week, before Cal's wedding had been delayed—though she told herself it wasn't to impress anyone. She needed something new, that was all. "And I thought we should discuss what to do before the wedding, so we can plan."

Louisa passed her mother's ruby-flashed serving plate to Grace Whitlow. "Have another little sandwich. It's a new recipe, chicken salad with crumbled potato chips."

"And very unique, too," Grace announced. "Maybe I should make these for the inn."

"You're still taking guests?" She supposed she should eat something, but she truly wasn't hungry. And her twin's odd recipes never inspired an appetite. Lou was fond of mixing all sorts of odd ingredients, and the results had led Ella to be cautious when accepting something new.

"Just a few," Grace replied, eyeing the sandwich filling. "And then I clean the rooms for the family for the holidays." She lifted her gaze to Ella. "So who is it, Ella? Gabe O'Connor was third on the list, after Owen and Calder. I don't believe that he would call you up and ask for a wife."

Louisa and Missy chuckled along with Grace, but Ella didn't crack a smile. Why wouldn't Gabe ask for her help, after all she'd done for his best friends?

"Not Gabe, exactly. Georgianna Moore." Ella plucked the folded letter from her skirt pocket while her sister and friends exchanged confused looks. "Maggie Moore's eight-year-old daughter," she explained, unfolding the letter and holding it at an angle so she would have the best light. "Dear Miss Bliss," Ella read, noting the extremely neat printing. "We need a new house and a new daddy. I here you are very good at this stuff. Thank you. Georgianna Johnson Moore."

"My, isn't Georgianna a pretty name," Missy sighed. "So old-fashioned and lovely."

"Let me see that," Grace said, so Ella passed the letter to her.

"Maggie's been cleaning out our attic," Louisa explained. "Sometimes she brings the children with her, but I didn't know that the older child was so, um, precocious."

"To think, a young woman like Maggie being forced to resort to buying and selling junk." Missy shook her head. "That husband of hers was quite a disappointment."

"We shouldn't speak ill of the dead," Louisa said. "But Jeffrey Moore wasn't the man his father was. And to think he was, well, you know, with Betsy Walker's daughter—"

"So sad," Grace agreed.

"Maggie gave us a very reasonable price for the old things in the carriage shed," Ella explained, hoping to bring the conversation back to the topic of matchmaking. "And she's making a list of everything in the attic, and then we're to mark what we want to sell and what we want to keep. She's a very strong young woman who really should have a nice man, don't you think?"

Lou sighed. "There must be a hundred years of junk up there in that attic."

"Junk?" Ella frowned. "It's not junk. It's our *history*, Lou."

"Well, our history is covered with hundred-year-old dust and could use some sorting out," she retorted. "And you tell me what you're going to do with a trunk full of old hats?"

"We could wear them to the wedding tomorrow," Grace said. "Vintage clothing is very in right now."

"It is?" Missy helped herself to another sandwich. "What kind of hats do you have up there, Ella?"

"Maggie will be at the wedding," she said, ignoring the question. "We should keep our eye out for someone worthy of her."

"Who?"

"I don't know," Ella replied, turning to her twin. They were as different as night and day, in looks and in temperament, and sometimes—very rarely, of course—Ella lost patience. "That's what we have to discuss. That's what I've been *trying* to discuss. Maggie will be at the wedding tomorrow, of course, since she was supposed to be the matron of honor the first time."

"I'd like to help the little girl," Missy said, wiping her lips with a napkin. "So why don't we ask her who she has in mind for her new daddy?"

"Until then," Grace said, pushing back her chair, "I say we take a look at those hats. We should look festive for the wedding, don't you think?"

"Festive?" Ella thought triumphant might better describe her feeling.

"Of course," Lou said. "We're all the guests of honor, aren't we?"

"I wouldn't go that far," Missy warned. "But I'm so happy that Lisette and Calder are finally getting married. Wasn't it nice of Mac to call and tell us!"

Ella ignored the giggles of her sister. "Robert has certainly been attentive."

"Very attentive," Louisa added, winking at Missy.

Ella thought that was a little unladylike and said as much.

"The hats," Grace reminded them, "are waiting. It never hurts to look one's best."

"Especially when one is attending a wedding, I suppose," Ella added, wondering if she still looked good in something with a wide brim.

"DO I HAFTA?"

"Yes. For the fifth time," Gabe told his son. "No matter how many times you ask, you're going to get the same answer. You have to go and you have to look presentable."

Joe O'Connor eyed the necktie as if his father had forced him to tie a rattlesnake around his neck. "I don't know why I can't stay home."

"We're going to Calder's ranch to see him get married. Kids are invited because his new wife has two girls."

"I know," Joe sighed, sitting on his father's bed and throwing himself backward while Gabe fiddled with his own tie in the dresser mirror. "She's in my school."

"Who is?"

"Cosette. What kind of a silly name is that?"

"French, I guess." Gabe eyed himself in the mirror and figured he looked presentable enough to be the best man. He and Owen, friends with Calder since high school, had flipped a coin to see who would do the honor. Owen had won last time, but the wedding had been postponed until Cal had convinced his bride he was serious about marriage.

"Georgie likes her."

Gabe turned to see the frown on his son's face. The boy had his mother's green eyes, but the rest of him was pure O'Connor, with dark curly hair and square face. "She does?"

"Yeah. A lot. She goes to her house to play with her sister."

Which meant that Maggie and her girls would be at the wedding, too. Heck, Maggie was probably part of the wedding party again. And seeing Maggie was always hard, even four years after the accident. Gabe stuck his index finger behind the knot of his tie and tugged, loosening the fabric so he could breathe better. "Try to behave yourself," he told his son. "Act like a gentleman."

The kid sighed. "I wish we could stay home."

"Not me," Gabe said, taking his dark suit jacket from its hanger on the door. "Our friend Calder is marrying the best cook in town."

"Better 'n you?"

"Yep. Much better. She makes pies and cakes and cookies and all sorts of fancy things. I took you to her store, didn't I?" He put on the jacket and turned to the mirror to make sure he looked okay. Not bad for a thirty-two-year-old father of two, not that he liked the gray hair that had somehow streaked his temples.

"No. That was Kate."

"Oh. I brought home something for us," he said, adjusting his tie so it hung straight. "Whatever it was was good."

"Yeah?"

"Yeah." He turned from the mirror and gave his son a gentle push toward the hall. "Let's get Kate and hit the road. I told Cal we'd get there early."

Kate stepped out of her room to show off her new dress.

"Dad? What do you think?"

"Very nice, Katie," he managed to say, because she looked older than twelve in an outfit that Owen's older niece had helped her shop for. Chocolate velvet, with short sleeves and matching stockings, replaced Kate's usual jeans and sweaters. She wore clunky high-heeled shoes instead of her usual riding boots, and her hair fell to her shoulders instead of being pulled back in a braid. His little girl was about to grow up.

"I've never been to a wedding before," she said, her dark eyes so like her father's. "This is really cool."

"It is?" Joe didn't sound convinced.

"It's a special day for Calder," Gabe assured

them. "And I know he'll be glad to have his friends with him to help him celebrate."

"Do you *like* weddings, Dad?"

Gabe tousled his son's hair and chuckled. "Sure," he fibbed, turning the corner toward his daughter's room. *As long as I'm not the groom.*

"Huh?"

Gabe didn't think he'd spoken out loud. "Nothing," he muttered, hoping Cal would be happy with his choice of bride. His two best friends had gotten married within weeks of each other, and Gabe knew that somehow the town's matchmakers were the reason.

He hoped they wouldn't be at the wedding. Between avoiding the Bliss sisters and pretending to act normal around Maggie Moore, Gabe figured it was going to be a long day.

MAGGIE, more comfortable in jeans and boots than panty hose and dresses, did her best to look good for the last-minute wedding. Her old friend deserved a sweet woman like Lisette, and Calder's transformation from wild bachelor to responsible married man and stepfather of two little girls was not something she wanted to miss.

"Mom," her daughter called from the bedroom door. "You look good enough. Let's go."

"Okay." She checked herself once again in the

mirror and hoped her red suit didn't make her look like Santa Claus. She'd tried to buy a new suit in Barstow two weeks ago, but nothing had fit, and the red silk suit in the window of Vintage Violets, a used clothing store, had called her name. Violet herself had even given her the suit at a substantial professional discount. She'd wanted to buy something new, she really had. She'd promised her mother that she would get something new—never worn, with price tags—for the holidays, but Agnes Johnson was doomed to disappointment where her only child was concerned.

Maggie tried twisting her blond hair into a knot at the top of her head, then gave up. She couldn't look sophisticated if she tried, not with an unfashionably curvy body and no skill with makeup or hair dryers. Most days she felt lucky just getting the paint off her hands. Maggie had short fingernails, bruises, chapped lips and no jewelry except her wedding ring, which she kept in the top drawer of her dresser.

"Lipstick," Lanie announced, joining her older sister in the doorway. Aged eight and six, her daughters had their father's elegance and their mother's looks. Maggie had no idea how genetics worked, but her girls were ten times smarter than either one of their parents. "You said not to let you forget your lipstick."

"Thanks." She grabbed one of the tubes lying on top of the dresser and applied something red.

"What color is that?" Georgie liked details, so Maggie turned the lipstick upside down.

"Hot Red Nights," she said, knowing the phrase wasn't going to describe her life any time soon. Maggie chuckled and tossed the lipstick into her purse.

"Cool," Georgie said, approving of her mother's outfit.

"I guess." Lanie, younger and more of a tomboy, wasn't sure. "You don't look like you, Mommy."

"That could be a *good* thing," Maggie said. She could be Margaret Moore, mysterious woman in red, instead of Maggie Moore, junk dealer and owner of More Old Montana Stuff. "Violet said I looked like a 1950s' movie star."

"Like Madonna?" Georgie frowned.

"No," Maggie assured her. "Not at all like Madonna. More like the movie stars that Gram liked when she was a girl." She hustled them down the narrow hall toward the stairs. They were clean, dressed and ready to go. She only hoped her ancient truck would cooperate. Cal's ranch wasn't too far away, but the Ford was barely holding together these days and, instead of putting more money into it, Maggie hoped to buy something else a bit newer.

Like the 1998 pale blue Chevrolet 4X4 that recently sat at the end of the road to the Loco ranch.

She wanted that truck. She had to drive by it each day for the past week and see it sitting there, unused and gleaming in the sun while she clunked and clattered and jangled past, all the while praying her old Ford wouldn't collapse in the middle of the road on the way to town. One of these days, she promised herself, when she'd sold more of the chippy white painted metal chairs or the rusted farm buckets so coveted by West Coast decorators, she would have the money for a down payment, one that was substantial enough to keep her monthly payments affordable.

"Get your coats and make sure you zip them up," she told her girls as she eyed gray sky through the kitchen windows. She hoped the snow would hold off until the wedding festivities were over. Marriage was hard enough without starting it in a storm.

MAGGIE IGNORED the best man as best she could, though one time her shoulder brushed Gabe's arm when he was forced to change position, when the justice of the peace announced that Lisette and Calder were man and wife and Cal moved to take his bride in his arms. Gabe, to make room for Cal's grandfather to extend his teary congratulations, had had to step close to Maggie or end up in the Browns' mammoth stone fireplace.

Maggie would have preferred that alternative, especially when Gabe looked at her and spoke. She'd assumed he'd keep moving, as they'd spent the last four years avoiding each other whenever possible.

"Well," he drawled, as the groom and bride embraced their families behind him. "I'd say they're going to be very happy together."

"I hope so." It was all she could think to say. Since she'd been twelve years old, standing next to Gabe O'Connor had pretty much taken her breath away. She figured now, when they were both thirty-two and grown-up, that her reaction was just habit, because being in the same room with Gabe was something she hadn't looked forward to in four years.

"I was glad to get the phone call last night," he continued in that low voice of his. Maggie looked at him and glanced away, but she had time to notice that he looked unfamiliar and formal in his dark suit, a handsome stranger with a wry smile and warm brown eyes. She gripped the bride's bouquet harder and winced when a tiny thorn pricked her thumb.

"Yes," she said. "I'm glad they worked it all out. She's a really nice person."

"And you've become friends," he said. "Obviously."

"Yes." It was all she had a chance to say because Lisette and Cal had turned to face them, and soon Maggie was enveloped in her friend's embrace. And then, after she'd transferred ownership of the flowers, she was hugged by a grinning Calder, who didn't look at all like a serious married man. In fact, he looked as if he was about to carry his bride into the nearest bedroom to make wild and passionate love.

Lisette was a very lucky woman. Maggie wondered if she could even remember what wild lovemaking was like.

"Surprised you, didn't I?" Cal draped his arm across Maggie's shoulders. "I'm glad you didn't have any other plans for today."

"Lisette said you two decided not to waste any more time."

He grinned and with his free hand reached for his wife, elegant and slender in a slim velvet dress of emerald green that Maggie couldn't have fit into when she was ten. "I didn't want to give her a chance to change her mind again."

"You were always the smart one," Maggie told him. "If you'd ever done any homework in high school you would have been class valedictorian."

"Someone else wanted that honor," Cal reminded her, and squeezed her shoulder. "You okay?"

"Never better," Maggie fibbed, suddenly wishing she could tiptoe out of the room and leave Cal's ranch. She didn't like remembering Jeff—not as the young man with all the dreams or the father of two, restless and bitter and discontent. "But I'd better go find my daughters before they get into trouble."

"They're hellions," Cal agreed. "But they're sure cute."

"Cal," Lisette said, frowning at him. "Maggie's girls are adorable and very well-behaved."

Maggie shook her head. "Your daughters are a good influence, Lisette, but Georgie and Lanie can get into more trouble than Cal, Owen and Gabe put together."

Lisette laughed, then looked for her girls. "They must be with Mac."

"*Grandpa* Mac," Cal corrected. "He's gotten particular about the title."

"I'll go check," Maggie said, anxious to move away from Gabe's silent presence. She could still smell his aftershave, a pleasant spicy scent that made her think of picnics. She turned to go as Gabe said, "Congratulations, again, Cal. I wish you two all the best."

He didn't sound too enthusiastic, Maggie mused. But then, why would he be? He'd had as disappointing a marriage as Maggie had. They'd both married the wrong people and tried to make it work—and then had been slapped in the face for their efforts. She found her daughters gathered around the dessert table, discussing which pastry they were going to eat first. Gabe's son figured he could eat six little éclairs at one time.

"No way," Georgie said, unimpressed. "You'll choke."

"I can," Joe insisted, turning to Maggie. "Mrs. Moore, can we eat now?"

"Not yet. We should wait for the bride and groom to lead the way."

"Shoot." The boy made a face. "These chocolate things look really good."

"Yes," Maggie agreed, eyeing the array of pastries arranged on glass pedestal dishes. Lisette certainly knew how to cater her own wedding. "Mrs., uh, Brown is a very good cook, but I don't think you should try eating six all at once."

"He'll choke," Georgie scoffed. "And then he'll throw up and make a mess all over the rug."

"Will not," Joe muttered, but he looked impressed with Georgie's prediction.

"Prove it," the eight-year-old said. "I dare you."

"Georgie, that's enough." She put her hand on her older daughter's shoulder. "Let's remember our manners, please?"

"Is there a problem?" Gabe asked.

"Your son's outnumbered, that's all," Maggie explained. "Six girls and one boy. He's trying to hold his own."

"Meaning he's about to get into trouble," Gabe said. He put his hand on Joe's head. "So maybe he'd better stick with his father for a while."

"Look at the cake," Joe said, pointing to a two-tiered cake topped with plastic fences and multi-colored cowboys and horses. "It's really weird."

Maggie chuckled. "Lisette said Mac ordered it to get her up here to see Cal. He told her he was having a party."

"And so he is," Gabe said, and Maggie forgot that she and Gabe weren't friends anymore. It was so easy to turn and smile at him. Share the happiness of two people on their wedding day.

Gabe began to smile, then stopped. "I wish them both luck," her old friend said. "Better luck than we had."

"I'm sorry," she whispered, unable to look away from him. He looked tired and handsome and terribly sad. "I didn't know—"

"No," he said, cutting off her apology. "You didn't, but I did. At least, I suspected—" He swore softly and looked toward the children. "Do you think we could put it all behind us?"

"No," Maggie said, which made his gaze drop to hers again. "It still hurts too much."

"Yeah," the man said. "But we could pretend."

2

"MAGGIE'S NEXT, you know," Calder said, pouring another finger of single-malt Scotch into Gabe's glass.

"Next?" He looked around the large living room, crowded with ranch hands and assorted friends, but he didn't see Maggie. And with that red outfit she was easy to see. Gabe wasn't surprised that Cal could gather so many guests with only a few hours' notice. He and his family were known for their parties. "Next for what?"

"On the matchmakers' list, along with you, of course." Cal grinned as if nothing tickled him more than to see his best man suffer.

"The festival is over," Gabe declared. "I think we talked about this before. We're all safe for another year."

"That's not what I heard," Cal said, taking a sip of Scotch. "Ella Bliss just got through telling my grandfather that she had one more job to do. A special request."

"And what does this have to do with Maggie?"

Gabe's back was to the fireplace, as was Cal's, as they looked across the room. Lisette, glowing with happiness, served desserts to a group of chattering children, and Maggie, a pitcher in her hand, joined the bride at the table and began to pour milk into paper cups.

"She's next."

"Maggie isn't interested in getting married."

"How would you know?"

He shrugged. "I haven't heard of her going out with anyone." And in such a small town, he figured he would have gotten wind of anything like that, especially during the festival.

"She could have any man in the county," Cal said. "With that face and that body, it's amazing no one has made a move on her already."

Gabe didn't like the sound of that. "Maggie doesn't date."

"She could," Cal insisted. "If she'd ever take time to fix herself up, like she has today. Usually she's running around hauling junk."

"I guess she makes a living at it," Gabe said, but privately he wasn't so sure. He'd seen that truck of hers and wondered how it could last much longer. Her shop, More Old Montana Stuff, didn't seem to do much business, though he'd heard through the town grapevine that Maggie had some kind of mail-order thing going.

"She must get lonesome," Calder said. "What about you?"

"What about me?"

"You've been alone as long as Maggie has. Aren't you looking for a little companionship?"

"With *Maggie*?"

"Hell, no. She's like a sister to you and me and Owen. I meant that you might be wanting to settle down again, put a woman in that cold bed of yours."

"Have you gone and joined the Bliss sisters? You haven't been married two hours yet and here you're trying to talk me into joining you."

"And Owen, who's thrilled with his redhead."

Gabe was glad for the change in subject. "He's not here. Why not?"

"He and Suzanne were up all night with the baby. He babbled something about a tooth and a fever and a rash, so I told him to go back to bed."

"I remember those days." Carole had cried whenever Katie cried, but she'd done her best to live on the ranch and make a home. At least for a while, until after Joe was born and Carole declared she needed to go back to college and use her mind. He'd thought that a strange way to look at motherhood.

"Why do you suppose the old ladies are wearing those strange hats?"

"Maybe they wear them like war bonnets. You

know," Gabe said, taking a long sip of his drink. "Like they're celebrating their success with you."

Calder frowned. "I don't think so. I've never seen 'em wear hats with feathers and flowers before. You don't think they've gone crazy, do you? Mac's gonna be real disappointed if Ella isn't sane enough to argue with."

Sure enough, Cal's grandfather was deep into a spirited conversation with the rail-thin Ella, dressed in blue and sporting a hat that looked like a birdcage that had seen better days.

"Don't tell me that Mac is interested in Ella—"

"Lord, I hope not," Cal stammered. "Though Mac said he used to go out with her—or he tried to court her, he said—when they were young."

"She scares me. They all do, all four of them, wearing those crazy hats and looking around at everyone as if they're sizing us all up. Poor Maggie. I wish they'd leave her alone." Gabe saw Maggie laugh at something his son said.

"She was too good for a jerk like Jeff Moore," Cal muttered. "It's really a shame that whole thing blew up in her face. Did you two ever talk about it?"

"No." What do you say to the woman whose husband had an affair with your wife, an affair you didn't discover until she and her boyfriend were killed on the road home from a motel?

"I'd forgotten how pretty she was. Is," he corrected, noting that voluptuous body. It didn't seem right to notice Maggie's breasts, though he'd have to be blind not to. Blond hair, blue eyes and a killer smile could make some man overlook the ramshackle farmhouse and barn full of junk Maggie called antiques.

"Yeah. The matchmakers will have an easy time of it," Cal declared, touching his glass to Gabe's in a toast. "To happily ever after."

"For whom?"

Cal grinned even wider. "For whoever wants it, O'Connor. You don't have to look so nervous."

Yeah, he did. Gabe wondered if he should warn Maggie that the matchmakers had something up their sleeves, that she was the next target for a wedding ceremony, an excuse for the women to wear hats and congratulate themselves for doing something that wasn't any of their business in the first place. He'd always had a soft spot for Maggie when she was Maggie Johnson and his next-door neighbor. He'd teased her during elementary school, ignored her in junior high, teased her too much in high school. He might have asked her out if he'd thought she wouldn't laugh.

No, who Maggie dated or slept with or married was none of his business. She wouldn't welcome his interference, he decided, as Cal's attention was claimed by Grace Whitlow.

He listened, just in case the woman—wearing pink lace and white flowers on her head—mentioned Maggie, but Grace was busy thanking Cal for the donation for the new church roof. Not only was Cal married, now he'd become a local philanthropist. Gabe decided to check on his kids, mostly to make sure that Joe wasn't showing off for the girls. If nothing else, he was going to eat so much he'd get sick on the ride home. Gabe downed the rest of his drink and set the glass on a nearby tray. Maybe it was time to head home before either he or his son did anything stupid.

"I DON'T RECALL asking for your advice," Ella said, enjoying herself thoroughly. Grace had been right about wearing a hat. It did give a woman a sense of mystery and excitement, and she liked the way the navy tulle tickled her cheek. Why on earth had women stopped wearing hats?

"You're going to get it whether you ask or not," Mac grumbled, his face and his bald spot turning redder by the second. "You should know that by—"

"Of course I know you're an opinionated old goat." And a handsome one, too, with that devilish gleam in his dark eyes. The Brown men had been lady-killers, every generation of them. "But you know nothing about matchmaking."

Mac waved his arm toward the groom, a man

who looked pleased with himself as his lovely bride joined him in conversation in front of the fireplace. "I did all right with those two."

"With help," she reminded him. "With a great *deal* of help."

"Doesn't mean you'll have the same luck with Maggie." He leaned over and retrieved a bottle of brandy from the coffee table, then filled Ella's glass and his own. "She's a special case."

"Very special," Ella agreed. "I wouldn't get involved with a new challenge so close to Christmas, but Georgianna begged." And Ella could never resist a heartfelt plea for help, unless it came from her sister. Lou was always asking for one thing or the other, so much so that Ella didn't even listen most of the time.

"The little girl wants a father, I suppose. Did she say who?"

"No, but—"

He frowned at her as if she was a novice. "Well, don't you think you should ask?"

Ella's eyebrows lifted, and the look she gave the man should have frozen him in his tracks, but Mac Brown was made of sterner stuff—or else was too old to be intimidated by anyone's looks. Ella turned and searched for the child, who stood to the side of the room and was busy wiping her fingers on a napkin. Ella caught her eye and crooked her finger, which had the desired effect.

"Yes, ma'am?" Georgianna said, a little out of breath from crossing the room at lightning speed. She looked at Mac and sighed, obviously thinking that the man was too old. Fortunately Mac had no idea that the lovely child found him wanting.

"I need more information before I begin match-making," Ella told her.

"Like what?"

"Is your mother, um, seeing anyone right now?"

Georgianna shook her head. "No way."

"Are you sure?"

"She works all the time. You know, like for you? In your attic."

"Yes," Ella agreed. "She works very hard."

"Lanie and me want a dad. Our dad died a long time ago, when Lanie was little. She doesn't remember him, but I do."

"Well, that's a good thing." Ella hoped the child's memories were good ones. No one ever figured out why spoiled Jeffrey, his college degree in hand, married Maggie Johnson, except that his father had just passed away and Maggie was the one who'd been hired to take care of the dying man. Grief could cloud a man's judgment, all right, not that a man would regret marriage to such a good-hearted and cheerful girl, but Jeff was a city boy, a young man who never intended to spend his life in Bliss. And Maggie was a ranch girl. It wasn't a match that Ella would have recommended, but no one had asked her, more's the pity.

"I like your hat," the child said, looking very much like a golden-haired angel. "Is it old?"

"Why, yes." Ella reached to touch the yellow bird perched on the side of the dark blue brim. "I believe it belonged to my aunt. My mother never cared much for hats."

"My mom likes old stuff." She looked at Mac. "Do you?"

"Sure I do," he said, giving Ella a wink that might have made her blush if she hadn't been too old for such nonsense.

"Do you have any idea what kind of daddy you want?"

"Oh, I *know*," the child replied, nodding. "He lives on a ranch. With horses. He has kids—a boy and a girl—and he cooks really good food, like pancakes. And bacon. And he has brown hair and a really shiny new red truck that doesn't make noise."

"My goodness," Ella breathed, wondering how on earth she was going to find such a person. "Sometimes—" she felt it necessary to warn the child "—we don't always get everything we want, dear. Sometimes we have to, um, compromise." She was in the middle of wondering how to explain the meaning of the word *compromise* when Mac cleared his throat.

"Well," he said, frowning at the child. "It sounds like you already know who you want. Like you already have one particular person in mind." He gave Ella a look she couldn't interpret, but the man didn't look happy.

"Yes," Georgianna said, shaking her blond curls and smiling at the old man. "He's always very nice when he visits our class, and Joey says he almost never gets mad."

"He?" Ella prompted, looking around the crowded living room. It was lovely to see so many people dressed so nicely and having such a good time. "Who is *he?"*

"There." The girl pointed across the room.

"Calder? He doesn't have children, dear, and I don't think—"

"Uh-oh," Mac said. "She doesn't mean Cal."

Georgianna giggled. "Not Cal," she said. "He's funny, but he's gonna be Cosie and Amie's dad now, not mine."

"Then who—oh, dear." Suddenly Ella was afraid she knew who the child meant. "Gabe?"

"Uh-huh. Mr. O'Connor."

Such a precocious child, with such an innocent imagination. It really was too bad she was going to have to disappoint her. "He won't do," Ella said. She'd never been fond of mincing words.

"Why?"

"Because..." There was no way to explain without revealing that particular scandal, but Ella did her best. "Because he doesn't want to get married."

"How do you know?"

"Well—"

"I could ask him," Mac offered.

"Okay." Georgianna looked at him as if she thought he was going to fulfill his promise immediately.

"O-kay." He gave Ella a here-goes-nothing look and headed toward Gabe, who looked like he'd had his fill of socializing. Ella didn't expect Mac to ask the man such an intimate question, but at least the child would be appeased when Ella had to explain that Gabe O'Connor would not be on the list of potential stepfathers.

"I don't suppose your mother knows what you're up to," Ella said, looking into a pair of innocent blue eyes.

Georgie shook her head. "It's a secret."

"I'm sure it is." Maggie looked especially festive today. It was too bad there were few eligible men here to admire her. "I'll do my best, but it is winter, dear, and a rather difficult season for matchmaking."

"That's when Mom said she'd get married."

"It is?"

"When hell freezes over, that's what she said." She shivered, illustrating the point that it was winter and cold. "My grandmother said that Bliss is hell when it comes to her artharitis, so—"

"I see what you're alluding to."

Georgianna Moore smiled, showing an array of perfect white teeth and a set of dimples. "Yep." She glanced out the window, where fat snowflakes fell past the glass. "It's hell and it's freezing and I'm going to get me a dad."

"NO, MISS LOUISA, I really haven't thought about getting married again," Maggie said as politely as she could. It was the third time the subject of remarriage had been brought up this afternoon. "Grace Whitlow and Missy Perkins asked me the same question."

"Now, Maggie, dear, you shouldn't frown like that." Louisa patted Maggie's arm. "It makes your face go all wrinkly, and you don't want lines, not at your age. Have I told you how nice you look in red?"

"Yes, you have, but thank you again." She wondered if she edged sideways and bumped into Lisette, would she be rescued? Plump, kind Louisa was a dear old lady, but Maggie didn't want the matchmakers focusing on her. She took a tiny step sideways, but Lisette had disappeared. "I'm glad you decided to wear the hats."

"Ella fussed, but when she saw how good she looked in blue, she relented. Now she acts as if it was all her idea." Louisa nodded toward her twin, cozy in conversation with Mrs. Whitlow and Georgianna. "She has a suitor again."

"Again?"

"Many years ago, when we were young—oh," Louisa chuckled. "I imagine you can't believe we were ever young, but we were. And quite the town beauties, if I do say so myself, though you wouldn't think so to look at us now." The fuchsia silk hibiscus flowers on her hat brim quivered. "Robert Brown— his family always called him Mac because his father was Robert Brown, too, and they were forever getting them mixed up—came courting Ella."

"He did?" Someone handed Maggie another glass of champagne, which she accepted gratefully before taking a sip.

"My father, bless his old-fashioned soul, didn't think anyone was good enough for his daughters." Louisa sighed. "In those days girls obeyed their fathers. Well," she amended. "Most of them did."

"And that's why neither one of you married?" Maggie saw Mac return to Ella's side and hand her a glass of something that looked like whiskey, then

Cal joined the group. Georgianna looked as if she was having a wonderful time entertaining the adults. Maggie hoped she was behaving herself. Sweet, outspoken, bossy Georgie never minded being the center of attention. Then Gabe's son appeared at her side and handed her a plate piled high with cookies.

"—making up for lost time," Louisa said, bringing Maggie's attention to her. "He's fond of me, and we're certainly having a lovely time keeping company together, though Ella doesn't seem to approve. But, as I told my sister, it's time to have a sex life, don't you think?"

"Absolutely." She took another sip of champagne and prayed that Georgie hadn't challenged Joe to a cookie-eating contest. Maggie turned and faced Louisa. It would be best not to watch, just in case. Did eighty-three-year-old Louisa Bliss just say something about a sex life? "I should probably check on the children," Maggie stammered.

"Be thinking of a man for yourself, dear. We'd love to help, and the girls need a father, I'm sure." She leaned closer and lowered her voice. "You're a young woman who shouldn't go to waste, if you know what I mean."

"I'll think about it," Maggie replied. She hadn't thought of herself as going to waste and certainly didn't want another husband, at least not one like the one she'd had before. It wasn't kind to think ill of the dead, but Jeffrey had taken her heart and pounded it into bits without even batting an eye. But going to waste? That didn't sound fun at all.

"Give us a few names and we'll do our best," the old woman promised before her attention was claimed by someone else. Maggie breathed a sigh of relief, then looked around for Lanie, last seen with Lisette's oldest girl.

"They're fine," Lisette said, reading Maggie's mind. "I settled them in one of the bedrooms with Cosie's dolls and cartoons on television. They were getting a little tired of all the noise."

"It's been a very exciting day for everyone," Maggie said. "How are you holding up?"

"I'm loving every minute," Lisette confessed. "I think everyone should get married."

Maggie shuddered. "No, thank you."

Lisette smiled. "I've heard that the matchmakers are going to work their magic for you. Shall I throw the bridal bouquet so you can catch it?"

"Toss it to Ella or Louisa instead," Maggie suggested. "It will make their day."

"Gabe O'Connor is a very handsome man," Lisette murmured, watching Cal and Gabe in conversation. "Why not him?"

"Why not him for what?"

"Don't pretend you don't know what I'm talking about. Why not you and Gabe?"

"I am never going to attend another wedding," Maggie vowed, wondering if everyone in the room had gone crazy. The festival was over, Christmas was only days away, and yet there was a conspiracy to marry her off. "Louisa just told me I was wasting myself and getting wrinkled, now you're trying to hook me up with Gabe. I'm too busy to think about dating or marriage or anything but kids and work."

"You don't have to get married," the Frenchwoman said, sipping her champagne and watching her husband. Gabe and Calder began crossing the room. "How about a romantic weekend together? He is a very handsome man and he seems so nice."

"Georgie's been hinting that I should take cooking lessons from my mother." It was her attempt to change the subject as the two men drew closer. Romantic weekends were about as far away from her reality as baking a batch of cookies whose bottoms weren't scorched.

"Perhaps I should give lessons at the bakery," Lisette mused. "What would you like to learn?"

"Engine repair," she said, wishing Gabe wasn't quite so good-looking. She also wished he hadn't married Carole Walker. "I think I need a new transmission."

3

"OBVIOUSLY we have to think of someone else for Maggie," Ella muttered. Mac didn't argue, but he didn't look too interested, either.

"Never mind all that now. We're going to do some dancing, Ella," he said, taking her elbow. "I fixed up a surprise in the old section of the house."

"What kind of surprise?" Ella wasn't fond of that sort of thing. She was the kind of person who appreciated preparation and advance planning.

He winked, reminding her how handsome he still was. "You'll have to wait, just like everyone else."

"Did you say dancing?" She looked around the living room, a nice enough space, if you liked rustic decor, but not designed for a fox-trot. "Where?"

"Just wait and see." He crooked his finger at his grandson, who took his bride's elbow and escorted her across the room to his grandfather.

"Mac?" Calder had never looked happier, for which Ella decided to take most of the credit. "What is going on?"

"A wedding needs music," the old man declared.

He raised his voice over the hum of conversation. "Folks? If you all would follow me, we're going to take this party one step further." Mac gave Ella his arm and led the wedding guests down the hall and around a corner to a wide wooden door. When he opened it, Ella saw a large rectangular room. An empty room.

"Go, boys," Mac called, and that's when Ella noticed a band set up at the far end of the room. They launched into some peppy country-and-western song Ella thought she'd heard on the radio, and before she knew what was happening, Mac swung her into his arms and two-stepped across the makeshift dance floor.

"Where are we?" she asked.

"The old kitchen and chow hall. The boys and I cleaned it out last night and hung some decorations." He nodded toward the patriotic streamers that dangled from the beams. "All we had was leftovers from the Fourth of July, but I don't think anybody'll care. It was easy to get a band on a Saturday afternoon, and I got Sam's restaurant to come up with some food, just in case folks got tired of munchin' all those little horse ovaries."

"Hors d'ouvres," Ella corrected, not certain if he was teasing her. She could never be too sure.

"Whatever."

"It's very nice," she panted, following the dance

steps but wondering if she was going to die of a heart attack before the song was over.

"Well, I didn't only do it for the wedding. I wanted an excuse to dance with you," Mac said, tucking her closer against him. Too close, Ella decided. Her sister might be acting like a cat in heat these days, but Ella knew better than to let physical attentions go to her head. She was too old for such nonsense, though she had to admit she had never danced so close against a man's body before. And Mac, old devil that he was, appeared to enjoy it.

She really didn't know what she was going to do with the man.

OF COURSE he would do it, to be polite. It wasn't such a big deal, Gabe reminded himself as he walked over to Maggie. The best man would dance with the matron of honor, as expected. Mac and Cal must have worked half the night to turn this section of the ranch house into a dance hall, and right now the bride and groom were dancing a cozy waltz, along with several other couples. It was time for the best man to join in.

"Maggie?" She stood in the corner eyeing an old worn cupboard shoved against the log wall, but turned when she heard her name. His daughter stood next to her, and he could tell by the look on Kate's face that she was having a good time. Without Owen's fourteen-year-old niece to keep her company, Kate was a little lost.

"It's gorgeous, isn't it." Maggie ran her fingertips along the crackled paint surface of the oldest piece of furniture Gabe had ever seen. Instead of glass, its doors were made of screens. "I was just telling Kate that you don't see many of these anymore."

"What is it?"

"A pie safe. I wonder if Lisette knows it's here. I think she'd—" She stopped when he took her hand.

"Excuse us, Katie," he told his daughter. "It's time for the best man to dance with the best lady." Maggie's skin felt warm, her fingers long and oddly sensual as they touched his.

"Have fun, Daddy," she said, looking as if she wanted to laugh at the idea of her father dancing. Maggie didn't look quite so pleased. In fact, she appeared flustered.

"You don't need to—"

"Too late." He led her to the edge of the dancing area and took her into his arms to begin the old-fashioned waltz. "I hope I can remember how this goes."

"Me, too. It's been a long time since—" Once again she stopped before completing her sentence. They both knew what she referred to, and Gabe was tired of the whole mess. Besides, Maggie felt good. Too good. He had to force himself to remember he was dancing with an old friend, someone he'd known since he was six, when she'd given him her peanut butter sandwich on the school bus. It was probably safer to pretend they were casual friends, doing the obligatory dance at a wedding.

"What were you and Kate talking about?"

"Painting buckets, packing up boxes," she said. "I could use some help right now, and she said she'd like to earn some money after school, if you didn't mind. She could also help me with mailings on Saturdays."

"She wants to *work?*" Lately Kate had started spending more time in her room and less time following her father around the barns.

"She probably needs some spending money for Christmas," Maggie said, adjusting her hand on Gabe's shoulder. He wondered if she felt as awkward as he did. Or as aroused. "We discovered we both like old things. She said her iron bed is her favorite possession because it has roses on it."

"Very old, chipped metal roses," Gabe said, smiling absently at Calder and his bride as they danced by. How long was the band going to play this damn song? "She refuses to let me buy her a new bed."

"The old one sounds lovely." She sounded as if she was serious.

"*Lovely?* It's older than her grandmother." He looked into those blue eyes and saw that she was laughing at him. Damn, he'd forgotten that Maggie was beautiful. And good old Maggie had breasts that could make a man—any man, let alone an upstanding member of the ranching community—beg for mercy. There were a few of Cal's ranch hands who looked like they wouldn't mind getting closer to Maggie, and probably closer than was necessary, if Gabe knew ranch hands.

"Haven't you heard that chipped metal furniture is very in right now?"

"I guess I haven't kept up with my decorating magazines lately."

"I can lend you some of mine."

He took the opportunity to tighten his hand on her waist. "Why do you paint buckets?"

"Because that's what people want. Really," she said, those big eyes of hers staring at him. "I could use the help."

"Fine. Kate's been moody lately."

"It's the age for it."

"Don't say another word," he said. "I like pretending she's still six."

"I guess denial can be good for a man," Maggie answered, making him smile as the song finally came to an end. Cal and Lisette, next to them on the dance floor, looked pleased with the music and the party.

"I didn't know getting married could be this

much fun. My turn," Calder said, releasing his bride to take Maggie's hand. "We haven't danced together since the senior prom."

"It was our first date and our last," Maggie told Lisette. "My date backed out at the last minute, and Calder's girlfriend, well—" She began to laugh. "Her father found out that she was going out with Cal and he threw a fit."

"So she—what was her name?—went to the prom with me," Gabe interjected. He'd forgotten all about that night, which had ended with a twenty-minute make-out session in the back seat of his mother's new Cadillac.

"Linda something," Maggie answered. "She moved to Denver."

"This is my dance, honey," Mac said, claiming the bride, so Gabe's relief was short-lived, because all of a sudden he found himself alone with Ella Bliss.

"Care to two-step, Miss Bliss?" He plastered a smile on his face as the elderly woman frowned at him and considered the invitation.

"Well, I suppose, Gabe, but I would prefer if we went slowly." She put her hand on his shoulder, and Gabe carefully took her right hand in his left and put his hand on her tiny waist. "Don't think I don't know what you're up to," she said. "And I have to tell you I don't think much of the idea."

"Pardon?"

"Her little girl might have stars in her eyes, but I don't think it's healthy, and I'm not going to promote it."

"Yes, ma'am." Gabe felt the beginnings of a headache hit his temples and thought he'd better start drinking coffee. He was too old to drink hard liquor and not expect to pay for it.

"Lyle Lundberg just built that big house right outside of town, you know, and I hear he's looking to settle down and start a family."

"Miss Bliss, what are we talking about?"

"Don't play innocent with me," the woman said. "I'll bet my last nickel that Calder has already told you we're about to work on finding a nice husband for Maggie. Mac tells him things that shouldn't be discussed, but that old man never could keep a secret."

"Yes, ma'am." This was none of his business, Gabe reminded himself. If Maggie married Lundberg and gave birth to lots of little future pharmacists, it had nothing to do with him.

"Your flirting with her isn't going to accomplish anything."

"I wasn't flirting," he said. "But—"

"You're the biggest flirt in town," Ella said. "Oh, not that you're out carousing like Calder, but you have that smile—plus a ranch that actually turns a profit. Every single woman in the county has hoped that you'd look her way, but you never go out with anyone more than twice."

"That's not a crime." In fact, he thought it was pretty damn fair. He didn't want a *relationship*, just female companionship once in a while. "I don't flirt," he insisted. "And I don't want a wife."

"Well," Ella admitted, "you've been treated poorly, so I suppose that's natural."

He would get even with Calder for this one day. Soon. Until then he'd try to change the subject back to Maggie. "Does Maggie *want* to get married again?"

"Why wouldn't she?" The lines on Ella's face softened. "Living alone in that ramshackle farmhouse, trying to make ends meet by cleaning out attics and dealing in junk." Ella sighed. "What kind of a life is that for a decent woman with two children? She deserves better, especially after being married to Jeffrey."

He supposed she did. He'd had no idea that Maggie's financial situation was so precarious, but he should have realized it when he saw her driving that truck, which was crap on wheels as far as Gabe was concerned. "But Lundberg? Maggie could do better."

"Well, there's Dr. McGregor. He's a little older than she is—"

"By about fifteen years," Gabe interjected.

"But just the same, at least he's settled financially and would make a good father for those girls."

If he didn't drink like a fish and have a girlfriend who was an exotic dancer, Gabe supposed, but he kept his mouth shut.

"And the new veterinarian. Louisa's always been allergic to animals, but Missy said he's very gentle with her little dog, that little fluffy thing with a flat nose that barks all the time. You know what I mean. Some kind of foreign breed."

"Pekingese?"

"That's it—watch out, here comes Mac, and he has no depth perception."

Gabe swung her out of harm's way. "The vet's a little young." He felt obligated to point that out.

"She can train him." Ella looked over to where Maggie and Calder negotiated a complicated twirl. She frowned at Gabe. "You're not interested in her for yourself, are you?"

"Miss Ella, I'd have to be half-dead and trussed up like a Christmas turkey to agree to love, honor and cherish again."

"Well, your wife was no prize, either," she agreed. "She and Jeffrey deserved each other, but we won't speak ill of the dead."

Not in front of the children, anyway. Carole hadn't been the most devoted mother in Montana, but the children had loved her. And Gabe had thought he did, for a while, anyway. When the song ended in a loud flourish of guitars, Gabe released Ella Bliss and hurried her to Mac's side. Let the old biddy bother someone her own age.

"Gabe?" Cal handed him a cold beer. "You look like you could use it."

"You have no idea."

His friend grinned. "Is Miss Ella matchmaking again?"

"Not for me." He took a long swallow of Sam Adams and felt the tension in his head ease. "But Maggie had better watch out."

"Our Mag can take care of herself," Calder said, and they both watched as one of Cal's younger ranch hands swept Maggie onto the dance floor. "She looks good when she gets dressed up."

"She's in trouble," Gabe muttered. "And she doesn't even know it."

"Maggie's no fool," Cal said. "And I'll bet she gets tired of being alone all the time."

"Yeah." He knew all about being alone. "Tell me about it."

"Maybe it's time you started looking around for someone permanent," Calder suggested with all the confidence of a recently married man.

"Women are trouble," Gabe said, expecting the groom to disagree.

"Of course they are," Cal replied, clapping his

hand on his friend's shoulder. "It's just that some are worth it and some aren't."

THEY WERE GOING to have a pajama party while the bride and groom celebrated their wedding night.

Maggie had had a lovely time, the best time in years. And now, her truck loaded with girls, she began the short trip home. Georgie, as the oldest, had the place of honor in the front seat, while Lanie, Cosette and Amie were tucked neatly on the small bench seat behind them.

The giggling drowned out the noise the truck made as it clanked down the road toward home. *Come on, you big old beast, just a few more weeks until I sell the saddle and the strawberry pincushion and the money comes in from—*

"Mommy!"

"What, Lane?"

"It's getting noisy again," she shouted, directly into her mother's right ear, making Maggie wince. "Is it gonna break like last time?"

"I hope not." The snowflakes, which had stopped for a while, had begun again right before they left the party with most of the other guests. Just flurries, but they still darkened the afternoon and made it look later than it really was. "We should get another thousand miles out of this old thing, if we're lucky."

"Are we lucky?" Georgie asked, peering at the snow beating at the windshield.

"Oh, absolutely," Maggie said, thinking of the wedding. Her new suit had been worth every penny—all seventeen dollars and eighty-nine cents worth of red silk and pearl buttons. She'd danced and laughed and even drank champagne—but not too much, knowing she'd be driving children home and taking care of four rambunctious girls for the rest of the afternoon and night.

"Mommy," Georgie warned. "What's going on?"

"I think it's the muffler," Maggie said, as if an eight-year-old would understand. "Open your window and let some fresh air inside."

"Why?" She did as she was told.

"So we don't have a bad smell in the car." She rolled her window down halfway and told the girls in the back to make sure their coats were buttoned. "We'll be home in a few minutes," she told them. "You won't be cold for very long."

She didn't think they paid the least bit of attention to her, as the giggling continued. At least Lisette's daughters weren't worried about having a new daddy. The children appeared to take the changes in their life in stride. Maggie couldn't imagine her children accepting a stepfather into their lives, which made the matchmakers' intentions all the more odd. Why did anyone think Maggie needed another complication in her life?

"Someone's behind us!" Lanie cried.

"The sheriff?"

"Who's that?" Cosette or Amie asked.

"Silly! Mommy wasn't goin' fast."

Maggie glanced in her rearview mirror, but she couldn't tell whose car followed them home. "Maybe it's Grandma," she said, though she didn't think her mother would drive out of town when it was snowing. And Saturday was her bingo night.

"Nope. It's going too fast," her younger daughter said.

"It's Mr. O'Connor." Georgie turned to her with wide eyes as if she announced a visit by the president. Maggie parked the truck by the sidewalk to the back door, and Gabe pulled in next to her. No one had used the front door since the lock jammed, and she didn't think Gabe was an official guest who'd balk at entering through the kitchen.

"Is something wrong?" she called from her opened window before she stepped out of the truck. Joe grinned at her and waved, then hopped out, a pink backpack in his hand.

"Joe," she heard Gabe call, then the man got out of his truck at the same time Maggie got out of hers. The younger girls scrambled out of their seat belts and managed to climb out the passenger door. They squealed when the snow hit their faces, shrieked when Joe pretended he was going to throw the backpack into the old lye pot, giggled when he chased them to the kitchen door with Georgie right behind him.

"Sorry," Gabe said. "Amie forgot her backpack, so I told her I'd drop it off on my way home."

He wore a down jacket over his suit, and his dress boots were spotted with snow, but he didn't look as if he noticed the bad weather. The lights came on in the house, including the one that lit the way up the steps.

"Mr. O'Connor!" Georgie's voice rang out, and Maggie turned to see her daughter standing in the open door. "Joe wants to ask you something!"

"Come on in," Maggie said, just as casually as if he pulled into her driveway every Saturday evening. She looked past him, saw Kate peering through the back window of Gabe's truck and waved at her. "Both of you. You can't stand out here in the snow."

He didn't look pleased, but he motioned to Kate to get out, and the girl hurried to his side and looked at Maggie with huge dark eyes.

"We can't stay," he said, as if she'd asked him inside for dinner and a movie.

"No, but as long as you're here you might as well

come inside." She turned toward the door and assumed they would follow her.

"Joe won't leave unless I go in and get him."

"He wants to stay and play with the girls," Kate
informed her father. "So he can show off some
more."

"Don't worry," Maggie heard Gabe answer. "I'll
take care of him. Mrs. Moore has enough to do without dealing with Joe."

Georgie opened the door for them and smiled.
"Hi, Mr. O'Connor. Hi, Kate."

"Hi," the older girl replied, stepping inside when
Maggie gestured that she go first. "Wow."

"You'll have to excuse the mess," Maggie said,
noting that the various projects scattered around the
large kitchen might look a little strange. "I'm trying
to get everything shipped so people have their
things before Christmas."

Gabe hesitated in the doorway. He eyed the rows
of colorful sap buckets, the stacks of Priority Mail
boxes, the human-size roll of bubble wrap next to
the refrigerator. His gaze fell on the saddle, the one
she'd won at the church raffle a few weeks ago,
which was sitting in the middle of the dining room
table.

"Would you like to sit down?"

"Where?"

He had a point. Every white metal chair, ornate

and slightly battered, held something to be mailed. Or packaged. Or painted. "In the living room?"

"I'd better get going," he said, so Maggie told Georgie to find the boy, which left Gabe and Maggie to stand awkwardly together in the crowded kitchen for long moments. She heard the thunder of feet coming down the stairs at the other end of the house, and within seconds Joe appeared in the door to the living area.

"Come on," Gabe said. "We've got to be getting home." He ignored Joe's groan, but hesitated and frowned at Maggie. "You really should have your trucked checked. I think you left part of your exhaust system in your drive."

"I was afraid it was something like that." She wondered if she smelled like exhaust fumes. "I'm looking at new trucks this week." Not exactly a lie. She looked at vehicles a lot, but buying them was another story altogether.

"Good." He stared at the white flowered light fixture that hung over the table, then his gaze took in the cupboards, counters and floor. She would have explained that she was in the middle of learning how to install tile, if he had asked. And she could have explained proudly that the chandelier was Italian tole, out of a house in Bozeman, and that she'd rewired it herself.

"We like that blue truck on the highway by your house," Georgie said. "We're saving up."

"Georgie," Maggie warned, but it was too late.

"It already has seventy thousand miles on it," he said, his frown deepening as he looked at her again. "And new tires."

He didn't look at all like the man who had asked her to dance a waltz. "You're welcome to take it," he said. "And just pay whenever you can."

"Thank you, but no. I couldn't do that."

"Why not?"

"If I decide to buy it, I'll pay for it, right then and there."

His mouth twisted into a strange smile. "You always were stubborn, Maggie. Just so you know, the price is negotiable, lower than the sign on the windshield."

"Good. I'll keep that in mind when I'm shopping."

"Shop fast, Maggie. That truck of yours is in bad shape."

As if she didn't know.

"We'd better go," he said, collaring his son and motioning his daughter toward the door.

"If you want to work tomorrow, Kate, come over anytime after eleven." Maggie followed them across the room.

"Okay."

"Good night," Gabe said, but the awkwardness was back. Or had never left. Still, Maggie decided, closing the door after him, it had been a wonderful day.

She'd danced with Gabe for the second time in her life. He wouldn't have remembered the first time, the night of their senior prom, when Cal had spirited away Linda Somebody, the girl whose father wouldn't let her go with him, leaving Gabe and Maggie to fend for themselves.

He'd been tall and strong and every inch the confident star athlete, but still the same person who had helped her with algebra and chemistry, who had teased her about her crush on her seventh-grade biology teacher, who had given her Mandy, her first horse, because Mandy was old and needed a friend and a place to retire.

She'd never thought they would ever turn into adult strangers, ill at ease with each other or grieving for their unfaithful spouses and angry with each other as if it was their fault that Jeff and Carole had been having sex in Bozeman for more months than either Maggie or Gabe wanted to know about.

Maybe, just maybe, they could be friends again.

4

IT SEEMED like a long drive home, even though it was only a few miles. Gabe didn't know why he suddenly felt so alone, despite the chatter of his children. Maybe because his two best friends were both married, would be tucked in bed with their loving wives tonight and every night. Gabe wished them well, but he couldn't help feeling an unfamiliar twinge of envy.

The house was cold and dark except for the light upstairs, left on for Joe's dog, who was afraid at night if left alone for too long. Puff, a strange combination of sheepdog and Labrador retriever, barked with joy when they entered the house and quickly scrambled outside to do his business under the safety of the outside light that shone on a wide path to the barns.

"Daddy, did you have fun?"

"Sure, Kate." He loosened his tie and draped it, along with his sports jacket, over the back of a kitchen chair.

"You looked very handsome," she said, going into his arms for a hug.

"Don't grow up anymore," Gabe said, holding his slender child. He felt her giggle.

"I have to, so I can have boyfriends and make you crazy."

"That is not a nice thing to say to a tired old man."

"You're not old," she said, pulling out of his arms to scold him. "You danced with Mrs. Moore."

"Yes, I did." He wouldn't easily forget how good Maggie felt against his body. He didn't think he'd ever danced with her before. Or maybe he had, that night at the prom when his date had left him for Cal. "I danced with Ella Bliss, too."

Kate moved away to open the refrigerator and retrieve a gallon of orange juice. "Georgie likes her, but I think she's scary."

"Me, too," Gabe muttered, making his daughter laugh again. Kate didn't know he was serious.

Much later, when the kids were settled in front of the television watching a movie, Gabe put his oldest, warmest jacket on and went outside to check on the horses. The two men who'd worked on the ranch for as long as Gabe could remember pretty much took care of the day-to-day chores, but Gabe liked to walk around for a while before he went to bed. He felt restless and edgy and not at all himself.

And he blamed the damn Bliss sisters and their

friends. Maggie didn't stand a chance against the matchmakers. She was a pretty woman, smart and kind and probably lonely, too. Ripe for any man who could supply her with reliable transportation and take her out of that "ramshackle farmhouse," as Ella Bliss had called it.

The wonder of it was that Maggie hadn't left the place sooner, though she'd always seemed attached to that old ranch, come to think of it. But the truth was she hadn't had any choice. Everyone in town had known that Jeff's future inheritance had been spent on his father's medical bills and care during a long bout with cancer, so there would be no fancy house in town. Maggie had inherited a house from her grandparents, but there would have been all kinds of taxes and probably some loans to pay off, too.

It had never been a profitable ranch, being too small. While the Brown ranch was the kind of place movie stars wanted to buy, and Gabe's ranch remained a secure family operation, Maggie's home was the kind that people passed by on the road to somewhere else and wondered who the hell lived in *that* old place. Gabe couldn't imagine her attracting many antique hunters into the barn, its faded More Old Montana Stuff sign taking up one-third of the barn's south side. Maybe in the summer, with folks getting off the interstate around Bozeman to see what they could find, Maggie could make a living. But how Maggie made ends meet the rest of the year Gabe didn't know.

He could help her, though. He had sheds full of old stuff that needed to be hauled to the dump. He could pay her to clean it all out, and if she could sell that junk as antiques, well, good for her.

He didn't know why he hadn't thought of that before.

"WE SHOULD think about going to Brimfield in May," Aunt Nona suggested, looking up from the Sunday paper. "We could have us a booth, rent one of those big U-Hauls, camp with the kids right there with our stuff."

"Brimfield? Really?" The Massachusetts town hosted the largest flea market in the world three times a year, but it was a long way from Bliss, Montana. "That's pretty far away."

"You're developing a reputation, Margaret," her aunt said. "Especially in the primitive-country category. Might be time to meet some of your best clients."

"That's true," her mother said, sipping coffee. "One of these days you should go to California and meet the owners of some of those shops that buy from you. You could buy some *new* clothes for the trip."

She decided this wasn't a good time to tell her mother that she'd found a great pair of barely used boots on eBay for $6.99 plus $3.95 shipping—a bargain.

"Leave the girl alone," her sister fussed. "She looks fine just the way she is, and there's nothing wrong with wearing vintage clothing." Since Aunt Nona wore a pink silk sari and several long vintage beaded necklaces, she wasn't the best advertisement for buying used. Aunt Nona at sixty-three was eight years older than her sister and light-years away in personality, leaving Maggie to constantly wonder how the two women managed to live together. Agnes, a more traditional woman, preferred shopping at J.C. Penney and liked to buy new things, as long as she could afford to. Luckily she had a good job as a secretary at the town hall, so she managed her life as a widow without too much stress.

Nona lifted one strand of rhinestone beads to show her niece. "Nineteen thirties. Belonged to a dancer from San Francisco who retired to run a whorehouse in Idaho. What do you think?"

"Very nice. Can I borrow it sometime?" She had no idea where she would wear it, but the sparkle intrigued her.

Nona lifted the heavy strand from her head and placed it around Maggie's. "Take them now, for good luck."

"Good luck with men?" Maggie laughed. "Maybe I shouldn't wear something with such a wild past."

"It might liven you up a little," her aunt said. "Lord knows you could use a little more play and a lot less work."

Agnes shook her head. "I don't know what I'm going to do with you two. Come sit down and have some coffee, Margaret. And take off that ridiculous necklace."

"I like it," Maggie said, admiring the sparkling balls strung together with tarnished chains. "This is a good deal. I come to borrow your car and end up with a necklace, too."

"It's an early Christmas present," Aunt Nona declared. "She can't give back a gift, not to her old auntie."

"Old auntie my foot," Agnes said. "Sit down, Margaret, and tell us about the wedding."

Maggie checked her watch. "I'll have to give you all the details another time. Kate O'Connor is coming around eleven to help me with packing boxes, so I can't stay long."

"Gabe O'Connor's daughter?" Nona's eyebrows lifted to her red bangs. "How old is she now?"

"Twelve, I think. She was at the wedding yesterday and seemed like a nice kid. She likes old things."

"Does that mean that handsome father of hers will be bringing her over to your house?" Nona said, looking thrilled with the idea of a single man on Maggie's doorstep. "My goodness. You need to go home and change into something a little brighter."

Maggie looked at her worn blue jeans, insulated boots and navy sweater. "I'm not bright enough?"

"I don't like you in navy," her mother said. "Pastels would be nice. Or something taupe, with ivory silk tailored slacks."

"I got a lot of compliments on my red suit yesterday." She knew that information would please her fashion-conscious mother.

"Maggie looks good in black," Nona said, turning to her niece. "A long black velvet gown would be nice, with a low neck—you've got the cleavage for it, after all—and that rope of rhinestone balls."

"And where am I supposed to go wearing this outfit?" She held the coffee her mother pushed toward her and took a sip.

"There will be holiday parties," Agnes predicted. "I would imagine your new friend will host her share of social events at the Brown ranch."

"Maybe." She could picture Lisette cooking and baking and decorating—all with effortless skill. She would not be wearing something bright. She wouldn't break out in a sweat when her cookies burned up.

"Your friend Owen is finally married, but Gabe O'Connor isn't going out with anyone right now, is he?" Nona tapped her coral-painted nails against her coffee cup.

Maggie ignored the question. Before her mother could bring up the past scandal, she said, "Did I tell you that the Bliss ladies are trying to find me a husband?"

The burst of laughter that followed that question didn't do a thing for Maggie's ego.

"You think I'm that much of a lost cause?"

Nona shook her head. "Of course not, darling, but I can't picture you obediently dating anyone those Bliss biddies send out to the ranch."

"It is a little hard to visualize," her mother added. "Unless he was a truck salesman. Then maybe you might talk to him about financing or rebates before you kicked him out."

"Or the postmaster," Nona said, with a chuckle. "You see more of him than you do any other male around this town."

"I might surprise you," Maggie said. "Maybe I wouldn't mind going on a date every now and then."

Agnes recovered from that surprising statement first. "Well," she said. "It would be nice if you got out once in a while. Getting dressed up and going out for a nice meal does give a girl a lift."

"Think _cleavage_," Nona advised. "Think _Gabe O'Connor_."

Agnes scoffed at that advice. "Oh, for heaven's sake, Nona. Why would she want Carole Walker's leftovers _again_?"

And that, Maggie knew, was a question that had an easy answer.

HE FOLLOWED HER into the driveway, though Gabe didn't know the driver of the gray Oldsmobile was Maggie until she and her daughters tumbled out of it and Georgie waved to him.

"What happened to the truck?" It was the first thing that came into his head.

"It's back in the shop, waiting for another miracle," Maggie said, sounding as if she didn't have a care in the world. "I borrowed my mother's car. Hi, Kate."

"Hi, Mrs. Moore." Kate immediately left his side and hurried to her new employer. "What would you like me to do first?"

Maggie smiled. "Well, first you can go inside and get out of the cold. We'll go out to the barn later and start filling orders, but first we're going to get some boxes labeled and out of my kitchen."

"Okay."

"I'll show you," Georgie offered, taking Kate's gloved hand to pull her toward the back door. "Mom got up early and there's stuff everywhere. It's a real mess."

Maggie turned to Gabe. "How long can I keep her?"

"That's up to you."

"I can bring her home around five," she offered. This gave Gabe a chance to stride across the driveway and continue the conversation without yelling.

"That's fine," he said, wondering why all of a sudden he was nervous. He wasn't going to ask her out or anything like that, for cripe's sake. "I, uh, wondered if you'd look at a couple of sheds of mine that need cleaning out."

"Today?" Those blue eyes gazed at him in a way that made Gabe wish he'd stayed in his car.

"Well, yeah, if you have the time."

"I can take a look at them this afternoon," she said, hesitating. "Do you need them emptied right away?"

That was a good question. "Yeah," he lied, thinking of the condition of her truck. "I sure do."

"Well," she said, shivering as the wind picked up. "I'm finishing up the Bliss ladies this week. Did you want me to sell anything specific for you or give you a price for the whole lot?"

"I was going to pay for hauling it away."

She smiled, and Gabe realized he'd forgotten how pretty she was. "Well, that's a good idea, too."

He laughed. "Go on inside before you freeze, Maggie. I'll see you later."

"Okay." She turned and headed for the house, and Gabe returned to his car. There. Now all he had to do was figure out how to get her some decent transportation. While Joe was busy visiting his grandmother, Gabe decided to drive over and ask an expert.

"You just can't give her a truck," Owen said, leaning against the corral fence behind his horse barn.

"She can't drive that piece of crap she has now. It's December. She could break down anywhere."

Owen shook his head. "Maggie's proud. You can't turn up with a truck like she's a charity case."

"I don't know why not," Gabe grumbled.

"What's going on?"

"What do you mean?"

"You two have been avoiding each other since— well, for years. I must have missed out on something yesterday." Owen left the rail and turned toward the house. "Come on in the house. Suzanne will have coffee on."

"She won't mind company?"

"Nah. She likes it when you stop by. The baby's feeling better, so we actually got some sleep last night. Suzanne's sisters and their families are coming for Christmas. She's been cooking and baking and cleaning, so I'm not sure what we'll find when we go inside."

What Gabe found was a woman who wanted to hear every detail of the wedding, complete with the matchmakers' attendance and who wore what and who danced with whom and what the Bliss ladies said about the success of the festival. Suzanne had personal experience with the matchmaking success of the town's old ladies. The elegant redhead had come to Bliss to do a story on the festival and ended up married to the Hearts Club's first "project," Owen Chase.

"Tell me everything," Suzanne demanded.

"The matchmakers have a new target," Gabe grumbled, then wished he hadn't when he saw Suzanne's face light up.

"Who?" She pushed a plate of sugar cookies across the kitchen table towards him. "Eat all you want, just make sure you don't leave out the juicy details."

"I warned you," Owen said, reaching for a cookie. "You know, these are pretty good."

"Don't act so surprised," she told him. "And you warned Gabe about what?"

"Your interest in weddings."

"I'm writing a follow-up article for the magazine," she reminded her new husband. "I still don't think anyone at work believes I met and married a rancher just a few weeks ago."

"Have you met Lisette?"

"A few times. I've ordered all sorts of special desserts for the holidays from the bakery. I'm really sorry I missed that wedding, but I'm glad they got married, after all."

"So is Cal," Gabe said. "He was grinning from ear to ear the whole afternoon."

"Okay," Suzanne said, tucking a long strand of red hair behind her ear. "Who's getting married next?"

"Don't look at me." Gabe couldn't believe they laughed. "I'm serious."

"And so are the matchmakers," Suzanne said. "If they're after you, now that Cal and Owen are married, then you don't have a prayer. Who do they want to fix you up with?"

"You have it all wrong. They want to help Maggie now."

"Maggie Moore, the one with the antique barn?"

"More Old Montana Stuff," Gabe said. "That's the name of her business."

"I've been dying to get over there, but I'm not sure when she's open." Suzanne reached for a nearby pad and pen. "I wonder if she'd let me do a story on her. RoLi features businesses owned by women each month."

"Roli?"

"*Romantic Living*," Suzanne explained, writing something on the pad. "Does she know the matchmakers are after her?"

"Probably. They're not known to be subtle when they get their minds on something. In fact, Ella told me they've considered fixing Maggie up with the new veterinarian—that young kid, what's his name?" He turned to Owen.

"Doc Hathaway's not so young," Owen said.

"And Dr. McGregor, who's about forty-five, too old for Maggie, don't you think?" Gabe saw Suzanne write that down, too.

"Not necessarily," Suzanne said. "Some women prefer older men, especially if they're looking for a stable father figure for their children."

"He drinks," Gabe said. "Among other things."

Owen helped himself to another cookie. "Is Maggie running any animals out at her place now?"

"A couple of horses, I think," Gabe replied.

"Hathaway does horses, so that's good."

Gabe didn't think it was good. "Ella might have a lot of influence, but she can't make a horse sick just so the vet can meet Maggie."

Suzanne disagreed. "I think Ella Bliss can put her mind to just about anything and make it happen."

She leaned over, put her arm around Owen's neck and kissed him on the cheek. "Look at us. Who would have guessed how happy we'd be?"

"Should Gabe give Maggie a truck?" her husband asked, ignoring her question. He smiled at her, though, and Gabe figured the man was thinking of making love to his wife as soon as she stopped baking cookies and their company went home.

Suzanne dropped her arm and picked up her coffee cup. "Is this a romantically related question?"

"No," Gabe said. "It would just be doing a friend a favor."

"And she's asked you for this favor?"

"No. She's saving for a truck, saw the one I've got for sale and I told her to take it now and pay me later." Which sounded entirely reasonable, Gabe decided.

Owen chuckled. "You're only going to make her mad."

"I think it's sweet," Suzanne said.

"She's already said no," Gabe explained. "She said she'd pay for it up-front or she wouldn't buy it. She's a little stubborn."

"Yeah," Owen said. "A little."

"Well, you could bring it to her house and leave it there, with the keys inside, and tell her it was there to use in case of an emergency. Tell her it's there so you won't worry about her." Suzanne looked pleased with herself. "How does that sound?"

"I can't say that," Gabe said. "She'll think I'm coming on to her."

"And you're not?"

"Hell, no. I hate to see her getting stuck with some old doctor—"

"Or young vet," Owen interrupted, trying to keep a straight face.

"But otherwise I'll keep my distance," Gabe finished. Suzanne looked disappointed.

"Too bad," she said, doodling on the pad. "It sounds like she could use some help."

"I don't want to get too involved," he said.

"Of course not." Suzanne slid the cookies away from Owen and moved them in front of Gabe. "So just loan her a truck until Miss Bliss finds her a husband."

Somehow Gabe didn't think it would be that easy.

LOUISA ADMIRED the arrangement of white roses and baby's breath for what Ella decided was the hundred and tenth time today. Ella was surprised— and relieved—that her sister hadn't carried the thing into church this morning.

"I just can't believe I caught the bridal bouquet," she said again, inhaling the scent of roses as she bent over the dining room table. "I swear, Lisette tossed it right to me."

"Such a coincidence," Ella muttered, turning to the list in front of her. She didn't want to imagine her sister getting married and moving out of the house to live with the next-door neighbor, an aging gentleman who was nice but couldn't see well enough to drive a car without crashing it into something.

"It could be an omen." Louisa sighed, looking out the window toward Cameron's house, as if she hoped to see her loved one standing outside in the cold waving to her.

"Just because you caught something that was thrown in your face?" Really, Ella was running out of patience. And making a list of potential matches for Maggie Moore was not going as easily as one would have thought. Maggie was a lovely young woman, pretty and healthy and maternal, but she was also a little...strange.

"Have you found someone yet?" Louisa walked around the table and peered over her sister's shoulder. "The doctor and the veterinarian, good. Who's Rob Gladding?"

"The owner of an auto body shop outside of town. I called Grace, and she said he was thirty-five." Grace had also said the man was drop-dead gorgeous and had muscles the size of roasting chickens, but Ella didn't feel the need to repeat such an observation. "He may be my—our—best bet."

"Do you have a plan?"

"Not quite. Dealing with Maggie is not going to be easy. The man who gets involved with her will have to be very understanding."

"You mean about her house?" They both considered the worn-out, worn-down, falling-down-around-her-ears farmhouse.

"He shouldn't expect anything fancy, that's for sure."

"And then there's her work. He should admire a woman with her own business."

"Hauling junk?" Ella shook her head. "Maybe not."

"He must like children, old houses, antiques and—" Louisa hesitated, trying to think of more requirements.

"And Maggie," Ella finished for her.

5

"WHEN DID YOU want this done?" Maggie stared inside the second white-painted shed a hundred yards from the main house, a sprawling two-story home that looked bigger than Maggie remembered. She didn't know the last time she'd been at the O'Connor place. Maybe when Gabe's father had died, right after high school graduation. She and her mother had delivered a cooked turkey and chocolate cake.

"Whenever you can," Gabe said, his answer bringing Maggie's attention to the jumble of stuff piled to the slanted ceiling of the shed. She shone the beam of her flashlight and saw buckets, stools, chairs and assorted old unwanted bits of dusty furniture.

"The weather could make that difficult." The layer of dust made it hard to tell if anything was worth keeping, but Maggie never threw anything away unless she absolutely knew it was junk or checked the going price on eBay. "Are you sure you don't want any of this?"

"If we haven't used it in the last thirty years, I can't see why we'd want it now."

"Practical, as always," she murmured, wondering if there was anything worth saving. Or worth selling. And how she was going to haul it away if her truck wasn't—or couldn't be—fixed soon.

"I guess I haven't changed much," his voice was low, and she glanced over to see that he was serious. And that she may have hurt his feelings.

"Good." She met his gaze and smiled at him as if they were eighteen again.

"So that's a compliment?" The corners of his mouth tilted into a half smile.

"An opinion," she teased. "But if you need a compliment, feel free to take it."

"Thanks. You can't expect a Montana rancher to be anything but practical and thrifty."

"There's nothing wrong with either one," she told him, more aware than ever that they were alone together. And talking to each other again like old friends. Maggie looked at the shed. "I'm not sure when I can get to this. It depends on the weather, for one thing." And her truck, for another. "Are you planning on doing anything with these buildings right away?"

"I'm not sure."

"Well," she said, turning from the door so he could latch it shut. "I'll get back to you in a few days—or after Christmas, even—with a price and a time." She returned the flashlight to him and shoved her gloved hands in the pockets of her down jacket. "It's getting late. I'd better get going."

"Sure."

They walked in silence toward the house, their boots crunching on the frozen snow. Light shone from almost every window in the house, and smoke billowed from the stone chimney on the north side.

"It's a gorgeous house," Maggie said, realizing the place hadn't changed much since the last time she'd been here. The O'Connor ranch house was an interesting combination of history, practicality and additions made necessary by the growth of a large family in the past hundred and fifty years. Now it was all Gabe's, so the ranch was secure for another generation.

She hoped he knew how lucky he was.

"Thanks." She heard the pride in his voice. "I hope Joe or Kate will want to take over someday. I'd hate to see it leave the family."

"How's your mother?"

"She's fine. She moved to town last year."

"Does she like it?"

"Yeah," he said. "She does. She fixed up a set of rooms for herself when I got married, but she wasn't happy. She missed my father, but she stayed because Carole needed help with the children and wanted to go back to school—" He stopped in midsentence, and they both knew why.

"How long do you think they'd been seeing each other?" Maggie didn't expect Gabe to stop walking and turn to look at her. She couldn't tell from his expression whether the question was out of line, but she'd had to ask. There was no one else who would know, and after so many years, maybe it was time for some answers.

"I think it was going on for a long time," he admitted. "Maybe months. Or longer. She wasn't happy almost from the beginning. We had to get married, you know." Gabe frowned. "She was pregnant with Kate, and I was crazy about the idea of marrying her and having kids and raising them here like my folks did."

"I think Jeff always loved her." It was a hard thing to admit, but she'd had a long time to realize the truth. "He told me about two weeks before the...accident that he didn't want to live on the ranch anymore. I didn't know he meant he didn't want to live with me."

"Maggie, I'm sorry."

"It's not your fault. Really. I really thought he loved me," Maggie said, hating the way her voice broke. She never cried, and she sure as heck wasn't going to do it now, in front of Gabe. But he opened his arms and stepped forward, and her cheek was against the cold denim of his jacket. His arms enfolded her with a warmth that made her feel as if she wasn't alone anymore, at least not for this minute.

"I know," he said, his voice low and soft. She thought she felt the touch of his lips on her forehead, but she knew she must be imagining it. She wouldn't know what Gabe's lips felt like, though when she was younger she'd spent many nights dreaming about it.

"They didn't mean to hurt anyone, I guess," Maggie said, hoping to comfort him. "It just happened."

"Bullshit." He pulled away to look at her. He put a gloved hand on either side of her face as if he was afraid she wouldn't look at him if he didn't hold her. "Listen to me, honey. They knew exactly what they were doing, which was having an affair behind our backs. And if they hadn't gotten themselves killed, they would have torn both of their families apart and never looked back."

She didn't know what to say. She could only look at him and wish he would stop saying those things.

"Come on, Maggie. Weren't you ever angry with him? Didn't you ever wish you could scream and yell and tell him what you thought?"

"He didn't love me the way he loved her," Maggie said. "Nothing I could say or do would change that."

"I didn't know what was going on, Maggie. I suspected something, but I didn't know your husband was involved," he said. "If I'd known I would have—"

"What? Told me?"

"Yes."

"Why?" She couldn't picture Gabe deliberately setting out to destroy her. Not even because of Jeff.

"You didn't deserve to be treated that way. And neither did I."

His leather-covered thumb touched the corner of her lip.

"I have to go," she said, stepping back so he had to release her. She was cold again, and she wanted to go home. She wanted to be away from Gabe and his warmth, wanted to be anywhere but alone with a man she'd adored since she was a child. They'd been pals and buddies and cohorts. They'd taunted Calder and rescued Owen and grown up as wild ranch kids who loved the outdoors and suffered through high school.

She'd always wanted what she couldn't have. "Good old Maggie," the boys had called her. She'd wanted to be more than that to Gabe O'Connor.

Now Cal and Owen were married, and she and Gabe were alone. Tonight they had talked about their marriages. He had held her—briefly, warmly—as a friend. So why did she feel as if she had tortured herself again with what she could never have?

"I MADE plenty for everyone."

Gabe stood in the middle of his kitchen and was helpless to say anything to his daughter. Kate stood proudly by the stove, a huge skillet of scrambled eggs cooking on the front burner. She even wore her grandmother's faded calico apron.

"That's very thoughtful of you, Kate," Maggie began. "But we really should be getting home."

"Why?" Georgie asked. She put the finishing touches on the table settings and admired her handiwork. The forks, knives and spoons were ramrod straight in their assigned positions.

"Because we have dinner waiting for us at home," her mother explained.

"You said we were just having sandwiches," Georgie reminded her. "We always have sandwiches and potato chips on Sunday nights."

"Cool." Joe handed Georgie a stack of paper napkins.

"What do you guys have?"

"Breakfast," the boy said, telling the family secrets and not looking at his father's expression. "We always have breakfast for supper on Sundays."

"Where's Lanie?"

"Watching TV with the dog," her sister said. "She

really likes the dog. I wish we could get one." Those blue eyes, so like her mother's, gave Maggie a beseeching look. "Could we get a dog? Just a little one?"

"We can talk about this later—"

"You have to stay." Kate looked as if she was going to cry, a look that Gabe was starting to get used to. Owen warned him this was the age for it, but that didn't make experiencing it any better. "I cooked a lot of eggs."

"Maggie?" He waited for her to look away from the table, set neatly for six people, and look at him instead. "We'd like it if you stayed for supper." *Please*, he begged silently. *Don't disappoint Kate. Have pity on me, please.*

Her eyebrows rose, as if she knew exactly what he was thinking. "Well, then," she said, sounding cheerful and false. "Those eggs smell so good I guess I don't know how we can refuse." She walked to the sink and turned on the water. "I'll wash up, and then you can tell me how I can help you."

"It's all done," his daughter, the child who didn't walk until she was fourteen months old, announced. "And I made coffee. Decaffeinated, because that's what Dad likes at night."

"So do I," Maggie said, taking the dish towel Kate handed her. She dried her hands and told Kate how good the eggs looked while Gabe stood there and didn't know what to do.

"I guess I'll wash up, too," he said, heading out of the kitchen to the bathroom. He passed Lanie, with Puff in her lap, in front of the television. The little yellow-haired girl waved at him, and Gabe said hello. When he returned to the kitchen, all four children had gathered around the large table and all four voices were raised in conversation.

"Sit down," Kate said, showing Maggie to a seat at the foot of the table, opposite Gabe's usual seat. Georgie and Joe sat beside each other on one side, and little Lanie slid into the seat close to Gabe.

"Hi," she said, smiling at him with her mother's smile.

"Hi." The girls didn't look anything at all like their father, thank God. Gabe didn't know how he'd feel if they did. His hatred of the man who had stolen his wife had faded with the years but never really disappeared. These little girls took after their mother, lucky for them.

"I like your doggie," the child told him.

"I'm sure he likes you, too," Gabe answered, taking the heavy ceramic dish Kate handed him. It was filled with sausages, so many sausages Gabe realized Kate had cooked every single package he'd bought at the store last week. There had been a sale, so he'd stocked up.

Georgie and Joe argued about their homework assignment for Mrs. Barnhill and who could sing "The Twelve Days of Christmas" louder. Kate tried to tell Maggie about sixth grade's role in the upcoming Christmas pageant. Lanie fed Puff pieces of toast while the dog hid under the table and figured Gabe didn't see him. Maggie filled milk glasses, somehow managed to listen to three conversations at once and even found a way to eat the meal Kate had fixed.

There hadn't been this much noise in the house since last year's Super Bowl party. Later, as Maggie helped Kate with the dishes and Joe, griping and disgusted, was sent upstairs to shower and Lanie crawled under the kitchen table with Puff, Georgie took Gabe's hand and pulled him into the quiet living room.

"We want a new dad," she whispered, looking at him as if she waited for him to say something helpful and wise. Gabe opened his mouth and hoped the right words would fall out.

"Well," he said, discovering nothing to say that could possibly be helpful. "That's good."

"Yep." She continued to stare at him expectantly.

"I hope you get one," Gabe finally said.

"Yeah," the little girl whispered, leaning closer. "Miss Bliss is helping us. It's gonna be a real good deal."

He thought about that conversation later, when

the kids were in bed and he was alone downstairs, since Puff deserted him nightly for the rug beside Joe's bed. Georgie was a funny little kid. She and Joe had become pretty good friends these past months, since they were in the same class. He didn't blame the child for wanting a father, like he wouldn't blame his own children for wishing for a mother.

But just the thought of marriage made Gabe pour himself a small glass of Scotch and contemplate locking himself in the barn until any and all marital danger had passed. And he couldn't imagine Maggie wanting to marry again, either. After living with Jeff Moore, why would she want to?

"DO YOU THINK he likes us?"

"Who?"

"Mr. O'Connor."

Maggie stopped folding clean clothes into Georgie's dresser and turned toward her daughter, tucked in bed and ready—almost—for sleep. "What makes you think he doesn't?"

"He's kinda quiet."

"That's just his way." She walked across the room and perched on the edge of Georgie's bed.

"I like his house," Georgie whispered, and they both glanced toward the other side of the room where Lanie slept, a battered blue teddy bear tucked against her cheek.

"Yes. It's a very nice house," Maggie agreed as she turned out the light on the nightstand.

"Bigger than ours."

"Yes." And cleaner and quieter and much more organized. Gabe wouldn't understand the recent shabby-chic decorating style, would not come close to comprehending primitive chic or any furniture labeled humble.

"I like Kate, too," Georgie continued, snuggling deeper under her quilts. "And the dog."

"It was a very nice evening." She had the horrible suspicion she knew where this was leading, but she wasn't entirely sure. "Georgie, what are you getting at?"

"Nothing." The little girl smiled at her and raised her arms for a hug. "I had a good time, that's all."

"That's all?" She bent and kissed Georgie's forehead.

"Uh-huh. Are we going to see Miss Ella tomorrow after school?"

"Yes. I'll be working there till suppertime, just like I did last week, but you'll come over after school."

"Good." Georgie closed her eyes, but the smile stayed on her face. "Good night."

"Good night." Maggie left the half-finished laundry for the morning and decided she'd better keep an eye on her elder child. The Bliss sisters could very well be a bad influence.

ELLA BORROWED Missy's silly flat-faced dog and placed a call to the young veterinarian, a man she figured could certainly use the business, as he was developing his own practice in the county.

"I don't know, sister." Louisa wrung her hands and looked up the stairs as if she was afraid Maggie was going to come down from the attic and discover their plan. "You may have gone too far."

"I've only just begun," Ella announced, wishing Lou would stop fluttering. "If this doesn't work, we'll try that mechanic."

"Not Dr. McGregor?

"No." Ella didn't care to elaborate on what Grace had told her about the doctor's girlfriend in Barstow or how much liquor he bought each week. Callie, Grace's granddaughter, worked in a hospital and therefore knew quite a lot of that kind of behind-the-scenes information. "I've had second thoughts."

Lou didn't ask what they were. Instead she eyed the little dog Ella had left in its little plastic crate on the living room floor. "Do you think it's okay in there?"

"Of course."

"Maybe we should let it out and let it walk around. It likes to walk, you know." Lou knelt and peered into the crate. "You'd think it would bark, being in a little place like that."

"Miss Ella?"

"Yes?" Ella looked over to see Maggie at the foot of the stairs. She carried a large cardboard box and was sure to want to know if its contents were of sentimental value. Well, the timing was a little off, but they would have to make do. "Oh, Maggie, dear, come see what we have."

"A cat?" She set the box down and stepped closer to the crate.

"Oh, no." Lou chuckled. "Ella has never cared much for cats and says she won't be stereotyped as an old woman with cats, but I wouldn't mind having a—"

"My goodness." Ella hurried to the front door. "I wonder who that could be." She knew darn well who it better be, but the man who stood on her porch was not the one she expected to see. This really was disappointing. Ella had no choice but to usher him politely inside out of the cold. "Gabe O'Connor, my goodness."

"Gabe?" Lou echoed, looking at Maggie as if she would have an explanation. The young woman appeared surprised and a little pleased, which Ella thought interesting, even if Gabe wasn't the right man for her.

"Hello, ladies," he said in that deep voice, all polite and innocent. Well, he couldn't fool Ella, not for one Montana minute.

"This is an unexpected...pleasure," she said, crossing her arms over her scant bosom, but Gabe looked at Maggie.

"I'm heading over to the school to pick up the kids. Do you want me to get yours, too?"

She looked at her watch and frowned. "I didn't know it was that late."

Ella, who knew precisely what time it was, attempted to turn Gabe toward the front door. "I'm sure Maggie would appreciate your help with transportation. Please bring the girls here. No need to come in."

"Ella!" Louisa gave her a shocked look.

"I can get them myself," Maggie offered. "I lost track of time, that's all."

"No problem," Gabe said, looking at Maggie as if she was a nice sweet apple dumpling sitting on his dessert plate. "I can save you a trip."

"Well," she said, blushing. "Thank you."

Blushing was not a good sign, so Ella gave the broad cowboy another shove toward the door just as a younger man appeared on the front porch. Thank goodness.

"Why, look who's here," Ella said. "That nice young veterinarian." She opened the door to usher a very tall, very thin young man into the living room. "You're Dr. Hathaway, aren't you?"

"Yes, ma'am. Please, call me Ben," the man said, his eyes widening when he noticed Maggie. He couldn't have been a day over twenty-five, Ella decided. She'd hoped he would look older, but then again, looks could be deceiving.

"I'm Ella Bliss." She pointed to Lou. "My sister, Louisa, and a good friend of ours, Maggie Moore. Maggie's helping us sort the antiques in our attic."

"Gabe O'Connor," the rancher said, holding out his hand to shake the vet's. "I think we met a few weeks ago out at Owen Chase's ranch."

"Yeah," the nice young man said. "That's right. How's that horse of his now?"

"Doing just fine," Gabe assured him, which was enough animal chatter for Ella. She ushered Ben closer to Maggie, who did look quite fetching with her hair tumbled on her shoulders like that. One of the buttons on her shirt had loosened, which exposed a little skin. Not a bad thing at all, Ella knew, though distracting at times to the matchmaking process if the wrong person was looking.

"The little dog," Ella announced, pointing to the crate. "We're, um, dog-sitting and he seemed rather listless."

"Could you take him out of the crate so I could

have a look?" The young man had such a kind smile.

"Of course. Lou, would—"

"On second thought," Gabe interrupted, taking Maggie's arm, "maybe you'd better come with me, honey, just in case the teacher won't let the girls leave with me."

"I could write a note—"

"No. Get your coat, and we'll leave the ladies and their dog with Doc Hathaway."

Infuriating, Ella fumed. The man made steam come out of her ears. She watched helplessly as Maggie got her coat and left the house with Gabe O'Connor. Ella was left with a tiny white dog who looked more like a snowball than an animal.

"Oh, dear," Lou murmured.

"Never mind," Ella whispered, when the young man turned to hang his coat on the oak rack. "She'll be back in a few minutes, and we'll try again."

"No, not that," Lou said, holding the little dog to her chest. "I think the poor thing wet himself."

6

"GABE, for heaven's sake." Maggie inhaled a deep breath of cold air and stopped dead in her tracks on the Bliss front porch. "Why are you in such a rush?"

He turned, having started down the stairs, and looked back at her. "I'm not in a rush."

"What was that all about in there?" Maggie wondered if the man had lost his mind. Two days ago they weren't speaking to each other, and now he was offering favors.

"Nothing," he said, but they both knew he lied.

"I'm not leaving here with you until you tell me the truth." Then she felt a wave of panic wash over her. "Is there something wrong with the girls? Is that it? The school sent you over here to get me?"

"Hell, no, Maggie." Gabe's lips thinned into a frown, and he took the two steps back onto the porch in one stride. Before she realized what he was doing, Gabe moved closer to her and gripped her upper arms to hold her in place. His mouth—his gorgeous mouth—descended, and he kissed her. It was fierce and brief and not at all what she'd expected, but somehow her toes began to tingle, and other parts of her body began to defrost.

"There," he said, not releasing her. He looked into her eyes and frowned even harder.

"There *what?*"

He swore, which pleased her. She'd never seen Gabe angry or flustered or at a loss for words, except maybe the time in high school when Calder put fresh cow dung in Gabe's locker.

"That'll show those old women. He's too young for you, that's all."

"Who is?" She realized he still hadn't released her, so maybe there was a chance he would kiss her again. Or perhaps she should kiss him. Just to see if he would still frown when the kiss was over.

"Hathaway."

"The vet?" she said, wondering what the young man had to do with kissing Gabe.

"Don't be stupid," Gabe said, sounding more like himself. "It was a setup in there."

"Miss Ella was trying to fix me up with the vet? How sweet. I wondered why they had a dog in the living room." She didn't think the young man could kiss like Gabe, though. She'd always wondered what it would be like to kiss him, but the kiss had been over before it began. "Do that again, will you?"

"What?"

"Kiss me."

"Why?"

"It was interesting," she explained. "You've never done that before."

"Sorry," the man had the gall to say. He released her and stepped away. "That's not a good idea. The matchmakers are after you, Maggie. You'd better watch yourself, or you'll end up married to the kid in there."

She couldn't help laughing. "I can take care of myself. Really."

"They got *Calder* married," he said. "And Owen, which is really amazing considering the man didn't even date. They're scary once they get their minds set, and you've been alone a long time."

"So I'm so starved for attention and sex and male companionship that I'd fall for the first guy who's nice to me and buys me a steak dinner?" He was starting to annoy her, even if she did like kissing him that one time. And from the way things were going, one time was all there was going to be.

"Well," he said, hesitating. "Yeah."

"Maybe you should mind your own business." She shoved her hands in her pockets and pulled out her mother's car keys. "Maybe I wouldn't mind having dinner with someone who was older than eight and whose conversation would consist of more than what she did in school today. And maybe," she said, moving past Gabe so she could descend the stairs, "just maybe, a warm bed and a warm body beside mine might be kind of a thrill, you know?"

She didn't look at him as she passed. She dangled the keys in her hand and marched down the steps. She crossed the lawn to the driveway where she'd parked her mother's car. Once safely inside with the door shut and the engine started, she dared to look out the window to see if Gabe was still around.

He wasn't.

Maggie told herself she was pleased.

"SHE'S GOING to have sex," Gabe told Calder, who poured him a cup of coffee in Lisette's bake shop.

"Of course she is," Cal said. "She's a grown woman. A widow. She's been alone for four years—at least, we *think* she's been alone. She's old enough to have sex, Gabe."

"She was talking about steak dinners and beds and bodies."

"So? She's allowed. What's wrong with that?"

Gabe couldn't believe Calder was so unconcerned about it. "They're going to fix her up with Hathaway, who looks about eighteen—"

"At eighteen he would be at his sexual peak," Calder added, setting the pot in its holder. "You want a doughnut or something?"

"No, thanks." He didn't want to think of Hathaway, Maggie and sexual peaks. It made him feel queasy. "I told the kids I'd meet them at the café for burgers in half an hour. They're Christmas shopping." He glanced toward the window and noticed that Lisette had strung tiny white and green lights around the moulding.

"That's nice."

"I suppose I'll have to get a goddam tree tomorrow."

"We're putting ours up tonight," Cal informed him. "We're having hot chocolate and some kind of special pastry shaped like a tree."

"Very domestic."

"Yep." Calder grinned. "Married life agrees with me."

"I'm glad." Gabe meant it, too. He'd never seen his friend so settled. Too settled to get riled up over Maggie's men. Gabe tried again. "If she doesn't have sex with him, if she doesn't *marry* him, for cripe's sake, they'll keep trying to fix her up till before Maggie knows it she'll be hooked up with another jerk like Jeff."

"Not necessarily," his friend replied. "Maggie won't do anything foolish. She's not the type."

"She married Moore. Talk about opposites," Gabe muttered. "Anyone could see it would never work."

"Yeah," Cal said. "She married the wrong man and you married the wrong woman and now you're jealous as hell because she's starting to look around again. What does that tell you, O'Connor?"

"It's not what you think."

"No?"

"No."

Calder ignored the denial. "You'd better get in there and stake your claim, pal."

"Me?"

"Yeah, you. Who else?"

"I'm not interested in Maggie, not that way." Though he sure remembered how soft her lips were under his, how her breath had caught in surprise and how she hadn't moved away from him. Another inch or two and those breasts would have been touching his chest—through about four inches of clothing. But still, touching.

Cal snorted. "Yeah, sure, O'Connor. That's why you're acting like a bull who discovers he can't get into the pasture with the heifers."

"She's my friend, that's all." She was a friend he wouldn't mind kissing again—and touching. And more. Shit.

"Uh-huh." Clearly Cal didn't believe a word.

"I don't want to see her get hurt again."

"No one does," Cal assured him. "Not you, not Owen, not me. But she's free to pick her own men, whether you like it or not." Cal got up and fixed the Closed sign on the bakery door.

"I just don't like the matchmakers bothering her." Gabe stood and took his empty coffee cup over to the glass-topped counter. "That's all."

"Well," Calder drawled, an expression of amusement on his face. "You'd better ask yourself why you're so hot and bothered all of a sudden. Before my wedding you and Maggie avoided being in the same room with each other."

"I felt guilty about what happened," Gabe admitted. He picked up his Stetson and his leather gloves, but hesitated before leaving the bakery. "And I guess I blamed Maggie, too, which wasn't right. But I should have been a better friend to her."

"Maggie's got enough friends," Cal said. "Either go after her yourself or mind your own business."

Good advice, Gabe decided. From now on he would keep his mouth shut and his hands to himself.

Though it wasn't going to be easy. And this was the second time in two hours he'd been told to mind his own business. What on earth was the matter with everyone?

"MISS ELLA, you've got to be a better listener," Georgie said.

"I'll bet that's what your teacher says to you all

the time, young lady." Ella wasn't daunted by an eight-year-old with an attitude. She poured her a glass of milk and set it on the kitchen table in front of her. "Am I right?"

"Yes, but—"

"And do you listen?"

The child rolled her eyes. "Sometimes."

"Your mother's finishing her work upstairs, but she'll be back tomorrow morning to settle up our account, so she and I will chat again." And perhaps she would be able to convince Maggie to agree to give the veterinarian a tour of her barn. He'd confided he liked antiques to Louisa this afternoon, once they'd discussed the health of the little dog. Turned out the silly animal had a bladder infection, so Louisa had gone to return it to Missy, deliver the medication and discuss the latest romantic developments. Knowing Lou, she'd be gone until suppertime and come home with more news of the neighborhood than Ella could stand to hear over their pot roast and boiled potatoes.

"Thank you for the milk," Georgie said, taking a sip. "Are you gonna chat about Mr. O'Connor?"

"Maybe. Maybe not." She couldn't explain to the darling child that Mr. O'Connor would have to find his own new wife all by himself, because his wife had stolen Georgie's daddy from Georgie's mommy.

"But I want *him*."

"We don't always get what we want in life, my dear," Ella cautioned. Her father hadn't let Mac Brown on the front porch, having a deep-seated distrust of ranchers and cattlemen. And now look. Her father would be rolling in his grave if he knew that Mac and Ella were seeing each other sixty years later.

"Yes, we do." Georgie grinned at her, completely oblivious to Ella's stern expression.

"And you're so sure of that, are you?" Ella couldn't help smiling.

The sweet child nodded. "We had supper with Kate and Joey last night. *All* of us. It was so cool."

"My goodness," Ella said.

"And Mommy's gonna clean out their sheds, soon as she gets a truck."

"A truck," Ella repeated. "That's right, your old truck finally broke down."

"Uh-huh, but we're saving to buy a blue one. It used to be Joey's ranch's truck, but they got new ones."

"A truck," she muttered to herself, trying to remember where she'd heard about trucks and cars and a single man. "I'm sure your mother could use one."

"Oh, yes," Georgie said. "But we don't have enough money yet. That's what Mom says."

"Well." Ella eyed the house next door. It was coming back to her now. Maybe it was time her sister's ancient boyfriend made himself useful.

MAGGIE WASN'T a morning person, especially after not having slept much the night before because she'd been remembering Gabe kissing her and wondering if it was a fluke event or possibly—just possibly—meant that after all these years the man was finally noticing her.

And when that man was knocking on her kitchen door at six-thirty in the morning, when all she'd had the time or energy to do was brush her teeth and put the coffee on, Maggie didn't want to let him in. She pulled her blue satin robe closer around her and wished she'd never seen the foolish thing in Vintage Violets. It wasn't warm, but it made her feel like a movie star.

But not today, not at dawn, when she looked at Gabe through the door's glass window. He was windblown, his cheeks ruddy, and he looked as if he'd been awake for hours and had enjoyed every minute. She flipped the dead-bolt latch and opened the door.

"Maggie," the man said. "Good morning. Is the coffee on?"

"Yes. Barely." She stepped back and let him in. She could excuse herself to get some clothes on, but then he might think how she looked mattered to her. She didn't want him to get the wrong idea and think she cared what he thought. But she made a feeble attempt to smooth her hair and she slipped off her ratty pink slippers, which were not even close to movie-star quality, and kicked them toward the pantry door where the boots were lined up. She took two mugs out of the cupboard and filled them with fresh coffee, then brought them to the table. "Do you take anything in it?"

"No," he said. "Black is fine."

"You can sit down, you know," she said, wishing he wouldn't stand there looking every inch the Montana rancher, tall, sexy and strong and smelling like fresh air and hay.

"Thanks." He kept his coat on, folded himself into one of her iron chairs and eyed the large glass-topped table as if he was afraid it wouldn't hold his coffee.

"It's actually meant for a screened porch or a sun-room," she explained, sitting in a chair a careful distance away. "But I couldn't resist trying it here in the kitchen." The old room, with its white-painted walls and battered wood floors, seemed to cheer up in the presence of the ornate wrought-iron set. She'd hung floral bark cloth drapes on the two long windows that faced the backyard and made cushions of similar fabric for the chairs. Gabe looked around the room as if he was in a foreign country.

"It's real pretty, Maggie. It looks like you've done a lot with the old place."

"Thank you. I'll give you the tour some time after the sun has come up."

He smiled, a slow easy smile that made her think of kisses and sex and how very little she wore under the satin robe. "You always were a little grumpy on the school bus in the morning."

"I haven't changed."

"Yes," he said, his gaze flickering over her outfit. "You have."

"What are you doing here, Gabe?"

"I don't want an argument," he said. "But I brought you something. Because we're neighbors and because, well, hell. Just because."

Her head ached, and she wasn't awake yet—not really—and the children were going to wake up in about fifteen minutes and she would have to pretend to function. "Gabe, the caffeine hasn't kicked in yet, so could you just tell me what's going on?"

For a moment she thought he was going to tell her he couldn't live without her and take her in his arms and kiss her silly, but she quickly let that fantasy go. Romantic gestures weren't Gabe's style, and making romantic gestures to her, Maggie Johnson

Moore, was not a possibility. Yesterday's kiss had been a fluke.

A lovely fluke, but—

"Maggie," he said, looking at her as if she'd fallen asleep in the chair, "I brought you the truck. You can borrow it until yours gets fixed or you can buy it now."

"I don't need your charity, Gabe."

He frowned. "You need transportation. And this isn't charity. It's neighborly assistance."

"I thought we talked about this before." Maggie covered her mouth to hide a yawn. Maybe she was still asleep, and this was some sort of weird dream. "I can't—"

A horn honked outside.

"I told one of the men to pick me up in about fifteen minutes," Gabe explained. "I figured I'd make a quick getaway before you could get too mad."

"I'm not mad at you, but I don't need your help." She stood up, and so did Gabe.

"I'll go tell him to give me a few more minutes," he said.

"Just take the truck and go," she said, knowing she was being foolish. But she didn't want to take something she couldn't pay for. Her parents, who'd never had two nickels to rub together, had taught her that lesson. "Please."

The knock on the door gave her the excuse to turn

away from him, but the man who stood on her back step was no one she'd ever seen before.

And she would have remembered, Maggie decided, feeling exposed once again in the blue robe. She would have to burn the thing, or sell it on eBay and buy something flannel and plaid and very, very thick if she was going to continue to have visitors before breakfast.

"Good morning, ma'am," a tall, dark-haired, incredibly handsome young man drawled. "I hope I haven't come too early."

"Come too early for what?" She crossed her arms in front of her chest and decided that if the young man was a rapist or murderer, Gabe would protect her.

"To deliver your vehicle." He held out two keys on a ring and waited for her to hold out her hand.

"It's already arrived." She took the keys and looked toward Gabe, who had risen from his chair. "Gabe, this is really getting complicated and I can't—"

"And you are?" Gabe put his hand on Maggie's shoulder as if to make sure the visitor knew she was his, so Maggie stepped back and invited the man in.

"Rob Gladding." He ignored Gabe's frown and moved into the kitchen.

"You don't work for Gabe?"

"No, ma'am." His eyes were almost black, and he

had eyebrows to match and a face that looked as if he'd stepped out of a movie. "It's got to be about fifteen degrees out there this morning, but the truck started right up like a champ. It's got forty-two thousand miles on it, but you shouldn't have any trouble. I went all through it," he said, smiling at her as if he delivered trucks to women every morning.

"My truck?"

"*Her* truck?"

Rob grinned, showing perfect white teeth. "I own the auto body shop in town, and I'm trying to move some of the inventory. Mr. Cameron—the man I bought the place from—said Mrs. Moore here wanted to try out this truck."

"Maggie?" Gabe put his arm around her shoulders.

"It's a sweet little Toyota Tacoma, with an extended cab and a camper bed," Rob said. "That's the one, right?"

"No," Maggie told him. She handed him the keys. "I think there's been some mistake." Rob looked so disappointed that Maggie felt sorry for him. "Why don't you come on in and have some coffee and we'll figure this out."

"Thanks, ma'am, but I've got someone waiting to give me a lift back to work." He looked uncertain, but he put the keys back in her hand. "Keep it for a few days. Take it for a test drive and see what you think. And if you change your mind, you know where to find me. Day or night."

He winked at her, then turned and walked down the path to the driveway. Maggie shut the door, and Gabe dropped his arm from her shoulders.

"Who the hell was that?"

"He introduced himself. Do you want a refill on that coffee or are you ready to leave?"

"I think the matchmakers sent that guy out here," Gabe grumbled.

"I'm seeing Miss Ella today, so I'll take care of it." She took her cup from the table and added hot coffee. "You don't have to worry about it."

"I'm not worried," he insisted, but he took her free hand and halted her in front of him. She wanted to start laughing, because she would swear that Gabe had been jealous of the younger man and his sexy smile. She left her cup on the counter and waited. "I just don't think it's a good idea to let those old ladies get you into something you're not ready for."

"Like what?" It was a dare, and from the expression in his eyes he knew it.

"Like this." He tugged her against the full length of his body, which was an excellent idea, Maggie thought, even though he wore more layers of clothes than a North Pole explorer. His hands cupped her face, his large fingers tangled in her hair, and his mouth slanted across hers in a way that made Maggie's knees buckle. She lifted her arms to his waist for balance and gripped the lambskin pockets of his jacket when he urged her lips apart with his tongue, teased her with his lips, moved his mouth against hers as if he couldn't get enough of her, couldn't be deep enough in her mouth to satisfy him. His tongue was slow and hot and demanding, like making love with him might be, Maggie thought, when she could think through the passionate haze that enveloped her. He backed her against the refrigerator; she shifted sideways to get the handle out of her back. His body pressed against hers in a way that made Maggie remember her empty bed and her empty body and a way to fill both at the same time.

But he released her suddenly, left her alone against the refrigerator while they both caught their breaths.

"Kids," he said, and sure enough she heard their footsteps upstairs, heard the water running and the toilet flush. He picked up his hat, pulled a set of keys out of his pocket and tossed them on the counter. "I'll wait for Hank outside."

Maggie remained speechless, trying to calm her heated body and return to some kind of normalcy before the kids appeared in the kitchen. Gabe hesitated at the door, his hand on the knob, and looked her over from top to bottom. "Sweetheart," he said, right before he walked out, "that sure is one hell of an outfit."

"Thanks." After two trucks, two men and one very hot kiss, Maggie knew she wouldn't be getting rid of her movie-star robe anytime soon.

7

"TEA?" Louisa handed Maggie a china cup with the familiar scent of jasmine wafting from it. Ella preferred coffee and said so.

"Just a minute, Ella," her sister said. "I want our guest to be comfortable. Can I get you sugar or honey, dear?"

"No, thank you, Miss Louisa, but I—"

"So, what did you think of our new vet?" Ella asked, impatient and ready to get on with the important part of the conversation.

Now that Maggie was through cleaning out the attic, they wouldn't have many chances to finish what they'd started, unless they got lucky.

"He seemed like a nice young man, but I told you I just am not—"

"Not interested," Ella finished for her. "I know that's what you said yesterday, but I thought if you had some time to sleep on it, you might change your mind. Don't you have a horse or some other kinds of animals on that ranch of yours?"

"One horse," Maggie said. "One very *healthy* horse."

Ella poured her own coffee and joined her sister and their guest at the dining room table. "A man who can cure animals certainly comes in handy around here. And I'm sure he knows something about human anatomy, too."

"Ella," Lou warned. "You mustn't nag."

"I never nag," Ella insisted. "I simply state the obvious until everyone agrees with me."

Louisa sighed. "I know."

"Miss Ella." Maggie set her teacup on the white linen place mat and looked as if she was going to say something unpleasant.

"Oh, dear," Ella said. "You are upset with us. Was it the truck?"

"We shouldn't have done that," Lou agreed. "It was a little bit too forward of us, I'm sure, but our hearts were in the right place. And Cameron was so eager to help, because the young man is new in town and doesn't really know anyone at all. And he was happy to let you try the truck and give you a good deal on the price."

"I know, but—"

"And we heard Mr. Gladding was a very handsome young man," Ella continued. "Grace Whitlow had her brakes fixed and raved about him."

"More your age, too," her sister added. "Though

there is nothing wrong with a younger man. Or an older one, come to think of it."

"Let's not talk about old men," Ella said, noting that Louisa's gaze had drifted to the window where Cameron's car sat in his driveway. "What did you think of the truck?"

"I'm not sure," Maggie said, which Ella considered a very disappointing answer. "I'm going over to the auto body shop now and talk to Mr. Gladding. This morning I had no idea what was going on." She smiled. "Gabe said he thought the two of you might have something to do with it. So he was right?"

"Gabe O'Connor was there?" Now this was a turn of events she didn't care for.

"Yes. He brought—well, never mind that. Miss Ella, you have to understand that I am not looking for a husband right now. Maybe not ever."

"Such a shame," Lou said, clucking. "A waste, that's what it is."

"Miss Louisa—"

"Never mind her," Ella told Maggie. "She'll get over it. We had such plans, though. So many possibilities not yet tried, so many avenues not yet pursued. And I was so sure that the delivery of a truck would spark your interest."

"It was very nice of you to think of me, but I'm taking care of my truck by myself."

"I see." Ella paused, then decided to jump right in. She didn't have much to lose. "Tell me, where do you buy your prescriptions?"

Maggie frowned. "I will *not* go out with Lyle Lundberg, not for all the aspirin in Montana."

"He's building a new house," Lou whispered, as if she was afraid saying anything nice about Lyle would upset their guest.

"And I'm sure it's going to be a very lovely house, too," Maggie said. "But I have two girls to raise and a business to run and I'm just too busy to start dating again."

"Oh, dear," Lou said. "Don't be too angry with us."

"I'm not. Not really," Maggie said. "I know you mean well, but I don't think my daughters would appreciate my leaving them with a baby-sitter while I went out dancing with auto mechanics and animal doctors and pharmacists."

"I see." Ella wanted to point out that Maggie's daughters might like to have a father, no matter what he did for a living, but she resisted the temptation. It would do no good to antagonize the young woman, not when there was still so much to accomplish.

"I hope I haven't hurt your feelings," Maggie said, standing to leave. "It's just that I'm just too busy to be dealing with a relationship right now."

"Of course," Lou murmured. "Perhaps next year."

Maggie only smiled, in a noncommittal way, and lifted her jacket from the back of the maroon sofa. "If I don't see you before Christmas, I hope you have a wonderful holiday."

"We will," Ella assured her. "And thank you again for your hard work. I'll call you when we decide to clean the basement."

"Thank you for the tea. And merry Christmas."

"And to you, too, dear," Lou said, following her to the door. Once Maggie had gone down the steps, Lou turned and shut the door. "Well, sister, now what do we do? Georgie will be so disappointed."

"No, she won't," Ella said. "We're not giving up so easily."

"But Maggie said—"

"Never mind what she said." Ella sighed. She wasn't pleased with this latest turn of events. "I'm afraid she has her heart set on that rancher."

"Oh, my." Lou sat down and poured herself some more tea. "The scandal—"

"Is four years old and has to be considered ancient history now." Ella looked at the portrait of her father that hung above the fireplace. "I suppose we must start living in the present."

"You mean—"

"Yes," Ella said, turning toward her twin. "I suppose we'll have to see that she has Gabe, after all."

"I'LL TAKE the blue ones," Gabe told the saleswoman behind the jewelry counter at the Montana Diamond Mine. His mother would like those, after having lost her favorite pair of aquamarine earrings on a cruise to Nassau last winter. His mother sure enjoyed traveling, now that she didn't have a ranch to help run.

Which he should be home doing, too, but Gabe was too restless to concentrate on the account books or the stack of record-keeping waiting in his office. So he'd decided to drive into town and shop early this year, before Christmas Eve. It was only the nineteenth of December, but the kids would be out of school on Friday, and Christmas itself would arrive Monday. Somehow things seemed speeded up this year and just a little off-kilter.

He walked around the small store while the woman wrapped up the earrings. He paused in front of the large display of engagement rings and wedding bands, the store's major moneymaker, he supposed, in a town that considered itself a marriage haven. There were diamond rings of all shapes and sizes shining at him. He'd never bought one before; there'd been no money for a new diamond engagement ring when Carole was pregnant and they were planning a quick wedding. She'd been disappointed, but there'd been no way then, with beef prices down, to afford such a luxury.

Calder was right. Gabe had married a woman completely unsuited for ranch life, and all because Gabe couldn't keep his pants on or have the sense to use a condom. Carole had been just as eager as he was, more experienced even, but he hadn't wanted to think too much about her and Jeff Moore at the time. He'd been too damn pleased with himself for going out with the most beautiful girl in town.

What an ass he'd been.

"Mr. O'Connor?" He turned to see the saleswoman hold up a tiny silver package topped with about ten inches of red ribbon. "It's all set."

"Thanks. It looks real nice." He signed the charge slip, tucked the box in his pocket and off he went, determined to accomplish a great deal, determined to forget that the blue earrings were the same color as Maggie's shiny robe.

He had wanted to run his hands down her shoulders and over her breasts, which were loose and inviting under all that satin fabric. He'd wished he could slip his hands under the V made by the robe crossing over itself and thumb the nipples that were barely visible under two layers of fabric. He'd seen a strap of pink nightgown when she'd pushed her hair back; he wondered what Maggie would look like in silky lingerie with those blond curls cascading over her bare shoulders and—

"Mr. O'Connor," the woman called. "You forgot your receipt."

"Oh. Thanks." He took the slip of paper and tucked that into his pocket, as well, then headed out the door. There were toys to buy, a new saddle for Kate and a bike for Joe, sweaters and boots and warm socks, too. He would send his mother-in-law the usual holiday flower arrangement, since she'd moved to Barstow after Carole died and didn't like to fuss much with Christmas. Truth was, she thought Carole could have married better and never forgave him for getting her daughter pregnant.

Well, it takes two, as his father would say. He wished the old man was alive now to give him some advice. Gabe stepped outside into the cold air and looked at the sky. Snow, he guessed, and soon. Maybe some colder weather would cool him down...and make him stop thinking about waking up in the morning with Maggie, dressed in blue satin and next to him in bed.

"I'LL TAKE one of those little pear tarts, please," Maggie said, knowing that she didn't need the extra calories, but wanting to celebrate finishing the Bliss job and making a nice profit on the work. Lisette placed the tart on a heavy white dish.

"They're my favorite, too," she said. Lisette never looked as if she ate anything she baked. "I might even have one with you, if you don't mind the company."

"I would love it. Do you have the time?"

"The morning rush is over," Lisette assured her, stepping around the counter with a tray that contained coffee and pastry. "And Mona is still here, so I can sit down and have coffee with you."

"How are you feeling now?" Maggie was one of the few people who knew Lisette had suffered a miscarriage almost two weeks ago, when she was about to marry Calder the first time.

"Never better," her friend declared. "Though I'm looking forward to getting pregnant again one of these days. The doctor said there was no reason I shouldn't."

"Good. I'm glad." They sat across from each other at a corner table, and Lisette removed the food from the tray and arranged it on the small table. "You and Cal looked so happy at the wedding."

"And what about you?"

"I'm celebrating," Maggie said. "I just deposited a check from Ella Bliss for cleaning out her attic and one of her little sheds. Now I can go Christmas shopping without guilt."

"Congratulations. What are you going to buy?"

"Georgie wants books and art supplies. I'm surprising her with a desk that I'm painting in the barn." She took a sip of very strong coffee. "Lanie swears she needs new cowboy boots and a long list of toys and games."

"Are you going to Barstow to shop?"

"I think I can do it all here, though I now have a car that can make the trip." She debated whether to ask Lisette's advice. "I might buy a new used truck, if I want. Believe it or not, I have two trucks to choose from."

"Uh-oh," Lisette said. "Does this have anything to do with a veterinarian?"

"No. Why?"

"Calder said the matchmakers were trying to fix you up with the new vet."

"I told Miss Ella he was too young for me." Maggie smiled. "She was very disappointed."

"I'll bet. So where did the trucks come from?"

"Gabe brought one that he has for sale. I've been looking at it and hoping I could get enough money together to buy it, but it doesn't feel right to borrow it." Though her refusal had irritated Gabe so much that he'd kissed her. Thoroughly.

"What happened to yours?"

"It lost its muffler on the way home from your wedding, which was when Gabe found out that I'd been thinking about buying the truck he has for sale. I have a very mouthy daughter."

"I think they're all born that way," Lisette mused.

"I have to find out today if it's worth putting a new muffler on it or not." She had a feeling the answer would be no, though. It would be a relief to quit worrying about that old beast. She could start off the new year right, with something reliable, if not brand-new. If she was careful with her money, she could afford reliable.

"And truck number two? Do you have another secret admirer?" Lisette leaned forward. "Is there a man in your life you're not telling me about?"

Maggie laughed. "You won't believe it. A very *handsome* man showed up on my doorstep this morning and said he brought a really nice used Toyota Tacoma for me to try out. I just talked to him about it some more, and he told me to keep it for a few days to try it out."

"And here I thought living in Montana would be quiet and not very exciting. Who was this very handsome man?"

"Rob Gladding. He just bought the auto body shop."

"I'll bet my dough mixer that the Bliss sisters had something to do with it. They're trying to find a husband for you, right?"

"Yes, though I've tried to head them off—"

"You can't," Lisette said. "Look at me and Calder. Did you ever think that would happen?"

"Not in a million years, actually," Maggie admitted. "But look at you. You're both very happy."

"And what about Rob?"

"He left the truck and went back to town. Gabe was fit to be tied."

"You're blushing," Lisette said. "So I won't ask why Gabe was at your house this morning. How long have you known him?"

"Since I was six. Maybe younger."

"And the two of you never—"

"No." Maggie shook her head. "He always thought of me as a friend, one of the boys."

Lisette laughed. "I imagine you haven't looked like one of the boys for a long time."

"He never looked at me. Not like that." Maggie took another sip of coffee and decided it was time to eat the tart, calories be damned.

"That's hard to believe."

"He was crazy about Carole Walker. He always was." Maggie shrugged. "I don't think anyone else could ever measure up. She was gorgeous and smart and elegant, and I'll bet Gabe always figured she was too good for him." Until, maybe, he found out she was cheating on him.

"Was she nice?"

"Not really." She couldn't help smiling at the expression on Lisette's face. Her friend looked positively thrilled. "What's so funny?"

Lisette picked up her fork. "I think Calder and I will give a small dinner party," she said. "In honor of Christmas. I think you will wear something very low cut, so that a certain rancher will notice that you are no longer one of the boys."

"Low cut?" The idea was appealing. Vintage Violets had a rack of evening wear, though Maggie had never taken the time to look through it. And there were Aunt Nona's rhinestones, too, for dressing up.

"Black velvet," Lisette mused. "Men love the feel of velvet."

"I didn't know that." There was so much she didn't know, such as what to do about Gabe. And why he was in her life again. "My aunt suggested black velvet, too."

"Then it's settled."

"I guess I'll go to Barstow. When are you going to have your party?"

"Friday," Lisette declared. "We should torture Gabe at the earliest possible opportunity."

"You're wasting your time. He was in love with his wife," Maggie explained. "And so was my husband."

"I know," she said. "Cal told me all about it, but that doesn't mean you can't wear velvet and drive him crazy."

"I like the way you think."

"Good. Can I go to Barstow with you?"

"Sure." Maggie smiled. "We'll see how the Toyota truck likes the interstate."

Lisette shook her head. "Forget about trucks. This afternoon you are going to tell me all about Gabe."

8

"IF THIS is about the truck, then save your breath," Gabe said. "I'm tired of talking about it." He was tired of a lot of things, including sleeping alone. And the sight of Maggie standing at his door tonight didn't make him feel any better. She looked pretty and windblown; her nose was pink, and she smiled at him in a way that made him think that cavemen, with the reputation of hauling their women into the cave, must have had it pretty good. At least it was simple.

"You're not very cheerful tonight." She held up a square white bakery box tied with string. "I brought you a present. Does that help?"

"Come on in." He didn't want a present. He wanted Maggie, pink nose and all. The thought scared him, so he carefully stepped out of her way when she entered the kitchen. "Is that from Lisette's?"

"Yes."

"Why?"

"Because it was nice of you to offer me the truck

and because I really can't accept it. But I appreciate the thought." She shoved the white cardboard box into his hands. "So I'm saying I'm sorry I was cranky this morning and thank you and please take it back."

"Take it back?" He could do this, he promised himself. He could act like a friend, which he was, instead of a lover, which he wasn't going to be.

"Your truck, that thing you don't want to talk about but we have to whether you want to or not."

"But what are you going to do about your old Ford? Fix it up again?"

"No. I'm trying out the Toyota for a few days and if I like it I'll buy it."

He wanted to ask her if she could afford it, wanted to ask her if she thought that Gladding character was honest or not, wanted to ask her why she was in his house tonight and would she come upstairs and let him worship her gorgeous body, but Gabe said nothing except, "I see."

"Have an apple dumpling," she said. "And you'll forget all about it."

"I don't think that's going to help." He set the box on the counter.

"Hey, you can't blame a girl for trying." Maggie put her hands in her coat pockets. "I guess I came at a bad time."

"It's not you," he said. "Not exactly. This truck thing is real suspicious, don't you think?"

"Well, not—"

"I don't trust Gladding and I don't like the way the matchmakers are throwing men at you." There. Let her think about *that*.

"I know, but I've talked to Ella and Louisa about it, and they're going to stop. I can take care of myself, Gabe." She had the nerve to smile at him. "Really, I can."

"This morning I had you backed up against a wall. Is that what you call taking care of yourself?"

"It was a refrigerator," she said.

"Whatever. The point is—"

"You were trying to make a point?"

"Well, no, but—"

"I thought you found me irresistible." She was teasing him again, he realized.

"You shouldn't wear that blue robe when you have company." There. He'd warned her. He'd done his duty as friend and protector, and if he wanted to lean forward and kiss that soft-looking hollow under her earlobe, well, no one would ever know.

Maggie ignored his comment. "Where are the kids? I wanted to ask Kate if she'd help me out Friday afternoon, since school gets out early. I'm trying to get one last shipment off before Christmas."

"Kate's in the tub—which could last an hour—and Joe's over at the bunkhouse getting help with his math." Which meant, come to think of it, that he and Maggie were alone. And he remembered how her lips tasted that morning. "Will you stay and have coffee?"

"Well—"

"I'll even share the pastries with you." After he kissed her.

She smiled. "I already had some, thanks. Lisette and I ate before we went shopping in Barstow this afternoon."

He hoped she'd bought a flannel robe, so the next time a man knocked on her door she'd be properly clothed. So the next time he saw her he wouldn't make a fool of himself.

"And your kids?"

"Are at Lisette's. Cal picked them all up after rehearsal today, so I'm on my way over there now." She looked at her watch. "I'd better get going. It's almost seven and it's a school night. We shopped until late, then I dropped Lisette off at the bakery to get her car and then ran home to get your keys so you could pick up—"

He put his fingers on her lips, a light touch. Maggie always talked too much when she was nervous.

"Shh," he said, and then there was nothing else he could do but trace those lips with his index finger while Maggie stood there silent and wide-eyed, staring at him as if she thought he'd lost his mind. "I've been thinking about this all day, damn it."

Of course he had to step closer and kiss her, now that he'd announced it. He lifted her chin and ever so carefully touched her lips with his. And Maggie didn't seem to mind, though he could probably blame her acceptance of his mouth upon hers on surprise or politeness. No, her lips softened and welcomed him, and her arms lifted to fit around his neck.

And there was nothing gentle in his response, just an aching need that only having Maggie could fill. He slipped his hands under her unbuttoned coat, ran his fingers along a soft sweater until he held both sides of her waist. And brought her against him, though not so tightly that she would feel his erection. This was Maggie, after all. A kiss—hot and needy as it was—was one thing, but letting Maggie know that he wanted more than kissing was, well, embarrassing.

As if he was a man who couldn't control himself.

Maggie's fingers caressed his neck, and her lips parted when his tongue swept over them. He thought he tasted apples and cinnamon, knew he could kiss this woman for hours without easing the need to have her. She leaned closer into him, that generous body of hers warm and soft against his.

Tonight there was no refrigerator to lean against—the damn thing was eight feet away—so Gabe gripped Maggie's waist and lifted her onto the island countertop.

"Gabe—"

"Better?" That was all he could ask before taking her mouth again. She was at the perfect height for kissing, especially when her legs parted and he could move closer.

"Mmm."

He took that as a yes and wondered at his luck that Maggie was here and kissing him back. His counter had never known such excitement.

"Gabe." She kept her arms looped around his neck. "What are we doing?"

He thought it was obvious, especially since he'd been about to slide his hands underneath her sweater.

"Having coffee and dumplings," he said, sliding his mouth along the line of her jaw toward that intriguing hollow he'd fantasized about a few minutes ago. "Discussing that damn truck."

"And the weather," Maggie whispered. "Do you think it will snow for Christmas?"

"Sure." He felt her shiver when his lips tickled her earlobe.

"You don't really think we're going to—have sex on the kitchen counter, do you?"

Gabe chuckled, despite the fact that his fingers touched the smooth skin of her waist. Leave it to Maggie to come right out with a question like that.

"No," he managed to say, moving back a little so he could look into her face. Her cheeks were pink, her lips slightly swollen, and her blond hair looked even more out of control than usual.

"Good." Maggie looked flustered. She took her hands away from his neck.

"Unless you want to," Gabe added.

"I've never—no, I don't think that would be a good idea." She tilted her head just a little. "What's going on, Gabe? We haven't so much as talked to each other in four years and now—well, you know."

"I know," he agreed. He was afraid he did. "I guess I'm glad you're in my life again."

"I'm not in your life," she said. "I'm on your counter."

"We got carried away."

She gave him a strange look. "I used to wish you'd kiss me like that when we were in high school."

"Is it too late to start?"

"Yes," Maggie said, and jumped off the counter. "It certainly is."

MAGGIE TOOK the dress out of the bag and put it carefully on a hanger, but before she hung it in the closet she debated whether to wear it. She could take it back. After all, she'd bought it new. The tags were still on it, so the Crystal Boutique would give her the money back if she drove to Barstow tomorrow and said she'd changed her mind.

"You'll drive him crazy," Lisette had said, peering into the dressing room when Maggie tried on the black velvet dress. It had long sleeves and a low neck, and the hem stopped a few inches above her ankles, so she could dress it up with heels or make it more casual and wear black ballet slippers and tights. At least, that's what Lisette had pointed out. Maggie had opted for delicate black boots, an old-fashioned design that made her feet look almost petite.

She would drive Gabe crazy? Maggie doubted that, even though the man had been acting strangely since the wedding. She'd like to think that the sight of her in her vintage silk suit had inspired lust and longing, but she knew better. All the years they were growing up, even after she grew an embarrassingly impressive pair of breasts, Gabe had never noticed her. Not like that. He'd been her friend; he'd married someone else.

A fancy dress and a rhinestone rope necklace weren't going to change the fact that Gabe's first choice had been Carole. And Jeff's first choice had been Carole. And beautiful, smart, elegant Carole Walker hadn't been happy with one husband. She'd taken Maggie's, too.

And now Gabe was kissing good ol' Maggie Johnson.

He must be very lonely.

HE FIGURED he must be crazy. Once the kids were in bed and the house was quiet again, Gabe sat alone in his living room and tried to figure out what the hell he was doing. And why he was so hot for Maggie that he'd lifted her onto the kitchen counter, for God's sake. It seemed that he couldn't be in the same room without groping the woman, which meant he was either not cut out for celibacy or in love with Maggie Johnson. Maggie *Moore*. He didn't think he'd ever get used to thinking of her by her married name.

Jeff had been a real shit, but Maggie had loved him enough to marry him. That had been around three years after Gabe had married Carole and they'd settled at the ranch and had never even come close to making love in the kitchen.

If he was smart, he'd stay away from Maggie. But no one had ever called Gabe O'Connor a genius.

"YOU'RE IN FOR IT now," Calder said, not bothering to hide his amusement. "Lisette's organizing a Christmas party."

"And that's funny?"

"It is when it means that you and Maggie are going to be there Friday night, and I get to watch you suffer."

"This is the last time I ever ask you to meet me for lunch." Marryin' Sam's was crammed with people, and it looked like everyone had packages and lots of Christmas spirit. The only song coming from the radio seemed to be "Jingle Bell Rock."

"You're gonna be glad you came," the waitress said, overhearing his words when she came to take their order. "We've got us a turkey special with cranberry sauce and homemade dressing."

"How can I resist," Calder said, making the woman—old enough to be his mother—smile and twitter.

"Make that two," Gabe told her. "Thanks. And we'll take some more coffee, when you get a chance."

"Right, hon," she said, taking their menus. "Be right back."

"Women love you."

Cal grinned. "Yeah. It's a gift."

"Why would I suffer at a party at your house?"

"Because after all these years you've finally woken up and realized that Maggie—" Calder stopped when the waitress returned with the coffee-pot. They sat silently for a moment while she refilled their cups, then Calder took a sip. "Not as good as my wife's coffee, but she doesn't serve lunch."

"It's hard to believe you're a happily married man."

"Yeah. My grandfather is thrilled, except that he's gained four pounds. Lisette makes sure he has all the cinnamon rolls he wants, and when he's not home he's taking Ella Bliss to supper at the bowling alley."

"Mac and Ella Bliss dating," Gabe muttered. "I think the whole town has gone crazy." He rubbed his eyes. There seemed to be a dull ache through most of his skull. "Me included."

"What have you done?"

Gabe sighed. "I'm lusting after Maggie."

"So?"

"So, it's not going well."

"I can see that," Calder said. "What are you trying to do? Sleep with her or go out with her?"

"Neither. I'm trying to keep her from the idiots the matchmakers are sending her way. I'm just trying to be a friend."

"Trying to be a friend," Calder repeated, looking very much as if he wanted to start laughing again. "You're acting like a possessive, jealous man who doesn't want anyone else around his woman."

"She's not my woman."

"Then leave her alone."

"I don't know what's the matter with me. Maybe it's the holidays."

"Maybe you and Maggie finally got over what Jeff and Carole did."

"She loved him."

"Who, Carole?"

"Maggie. I used to see her once in a while at school or something. She'd look at that SOB as if he hung the moon. I could never understand it."

"No figuring women," Calder agreed. "But he's gone, and you're here, and on Friday you're going to be drinking champagne out at the ranch with all of us happily married couples. You and Maggie will be the only two single people there. Anything can happen."

"She could bring a date, you know."

"Yeah, I suppose."

"Or I could." Like maybe Ella Bliss wouldn't have any plans for that evening.

"Yeah, but you'll piss off Lisette. She's trying damn hard to see that you and Maggie get together."

Gabe shook his head. "I'm not looking to get married again. Once was enough. Besides—"

"Yeah?"

"Maggie thinks of me more like a brother."

"A brother," Cal repeated. "Are you sure about that?"

He thought of kissing her, remembered her sweet, passionate response and then her quick exit. Maggie had told him it was too late, made it clear she wasn't in his life. "Yeah, pretty sure."

"Well," Cal drawled, leaning back as the waitress set their plates in front of them. "I guess it's up to you to change her mind."

"She's always been pretty stubborn."

"Hell." Cal laughed. "Women change their minds all the time. You just have to be in the right place when it happens, that's all."

"I TOLD THEM if it happened again I would call their parents," Mrs. Barnhill said. The tiny redhead didn't take any nonsense from the her third grade class. Bliss Elementary was in the middle of rehearsing for its all-important Christmas pageant, and there was no time for foolish behavior.

"I'm very sorry," Maggie said, looking toward her daughter, who didn't look at all concerned. "What exactly did the children do?"

"He took my milk bucket," Georgie said. "I'm one of the ten maids-a-milking, and we have colored buckets. Mine's gold."

"But she sat on my crown," Joe said, his gaze on

Maggie as if pleading with her to understand that it wasn't all his fault.

"You said you hated it."

"Like who wouldn't?"

The teacher held up her hand. "That's enough of that. The show is tomorrow night. I know you're excited about the holidays, but—"

"Mrs. Barnhill?" Gabe stood in the doorway of the classroom, his Stetson in his hand. Snowflakes dusted the shoulders of his jacket, and Maggie was struck again by how handsome he was. Solid and comforting and the best kisser she'd ever known. She sighed.

"Come on in, Mr. O'Connor." Mrs. Barnhill pointed to the wooden chair across from Maggie and next to Joey. "We're discussing the fact that Joe and Georgianna can't seem to get along."

Gabe didn't look pleased when he turned to the boy, a younger version of himself right down to the waving dark hair. "You're fighting with a girl?"

"She started it."

Georgie shook her head. "Did not."

The teacher held up her hand once again for silence. "The two of them have been teasing each other for a couple of weeks now," she explained to Gabe. "Between these two, the math testing and the Christmas show, I'm getting migraines."

"It won't happen again," Gabe assured her. He turned to his son. "Will it?"

"Uh, no," the boy agreed.

"Georgie?" Maggie prompted. "No more teasing?"

"I guess," she said, then at her mother's frown added, "I mean, absolutely positively *not*."

"Go," Mrs. Barnhill said, waving them all toward the door. "And don't forget to do your book reports."

"Yes, ma'am," Joe said, but he grinned at his father. "Can we go get something to eat?"

"Mom?" Georgie beamed, obviously thrilled to have her mother at school. "Can we?"

"Good night, Mrs. Barnhill," Maggie said, gathering her gloves and purse. Lanie peered around the door, having been told to sit in the hall and wait patiently. Kate was with her, so when they stepped into the hall it was as if they were one big happy family, except that Daddy didn't look happy at all.

"Geez," he muttered. "That call from school just about gave me a heart attack. I thought it was an emergency."

"She gets dramatic," Joe said, talking about his teacher, Maggie assumed.

"Quiet," said his father. "I don't want to hear a word from someone who can't behave himself."

"He behaved just fine, Mr. O'Connor," Georgie

said, smiling at Gabe as if she was hosting her own party. "It's my fault. My mom says I'm too rowdy and I talk too much sometimes."

"Like now," Joe said, punching her arm lightly.

"Ha!" Georgie punched him back.

"That's enough." Gabe took Joe by the coat collar and moved him away from Georgie and her tempting grin. "You don't hit girls."

"I guess it's a good thing they've never been in the same class before now," Maggie said. Gabe looked as if he'd spent most of the day outside. His skin was ruddy, and he wore jeans and what looked like his oldest pair of boots. She found it hard to believe that last night he'd kissed her, just sat her on the counter and kissed her silly, as if he couldn't get enough of her. It had been pretty damn exciting for a mother of two.

"I guess you're right," he said. From the intense look he gave her Maggie realized he might be remembering last night, also. "What are you doing for dinner?"

"Well," she stammered, remembering that he had slid his hands under her sweater and she had spread her legs apart to allow him to stand between them.

"We're getting burgers at Sam's," Gabe said, stopping in the middle of the hall while his two children. "Come with us."

"Why?"

"Because you don't want to cook," he said.

"My mom *can't* cook," Georgie declared. "Ask Lanie, she'll tell you." Lanie obediently nodded at the tall rancher.

"It's not that bad," Maggie said, making Kate smile. The girl came to her defense.

"You do other things, Mrs. Moore, like make old things look really special again."

"Thank you, Kate," she said, touched by the compliment. "But there are times I wish I could bake a pie." That earned another shy smile from the girl. "I asked your father if you could work for me Friday afternoon. Is that all right?"

"Sure."

"Let's discuss it over dinner." Gabe lightly touched Maggie's back as if to propel her toward the double doors at the end of the hall.

Lanie tucked her hand inside Gabe's. "Mommy can't cook, but she gives good hugs."

"Yeah," the man said. "I'll bet."

It was a good thing no one saw her blush.

9

"WE WEREN'T going to bother with a tree this year," Louisa told the others. "But Cam insisted and came over with one and even installed it."

"Hardly seems worth the trouble for an artificial tree," Ella grumbled, but her sister paid no attention to her.

"It's very nice," Missy said. "It must give you lots of Christmas spirit."

It gave her a runny nose, Ella wanted to say, because the musty aroma had filled the living room for two days.

"Can you believe it's Thursday already?" Grace shuffled the cards but didn't deal. She set the deck aside and reached for another decorated Christmas cookie. "Are we doing gifts now or waiting until later?"

"We can wait a while," Ella said. The four card players exchanged small gifts at Christmas, and Ella wanted to delay it as long as possible. Other than her gift from Lou, this afternoon would be the only exchange of Christmas presents she and her sister would have. Missy and Grace had families, complete with grandchildren to fuss over, so this afternoon's get-together paled in comparison.

Missy set her coffee down. "Well, if we're not going to open presents and we're not going to play cards—"

"Who said we're not playing cards?" Ella wanted to know.

"We are," Grace replied. "In a bit."

"Well, anyway," Missy continued in that sweet voice of hers that sometimes grated on Ella's nerves, "I wondered how things were going for Maggie Moore. Is there anything we should be doing in the romance department?"

"She wants us to stay out of it," Lou said.

"Who does?"

"Maggie. She was here the other day and not too pleased about the veterinarian, though she supposedly is trying out the truck that the handsome Mr. Gladding delivered."

"He is a good-looking young man," Grace murmured. "Has the look of a movie star about him."

"Maggie doesn't want to date anyone right now," Louisa said. "No matter what they look like."

"Nonsense." Grace picked up her coffee cup and took a sip. "I saw her at Marryin' Sam's having supper with Gabe O'Connor last night."

"You did?" Ella didn't know whether to be

pleased or depressed. She wanted to help Georgie with her quest for a father, but did the child's choice of stepfather have to be Gabe?

"With the children," Grace added. "All six of them sitting in the corner booth having a great time."

"Oh, my," Missy said. "That was quick."

"Were they sitting together?"

"Maggie and Gabe, you mean?" At Louisa's nod, Grace continued. "Oh, no. Opposite sides of the table. Like friends would."

"Friends," Lou repeated, looking disappointed. "I don't like the sound of that."

"What do you expect them to do in a crowded restaurant with four children watching?" Ella didn't mean to be sharp with her sister, but she felt edgy, as if something bad was about to happen. Perhaps she should telephone Mac later, to make sure he was in good health. No, that was ridiculous. The old man would think she'd lost her mind.

Louisa shrugged. "I hoped they would look happy to be together."

"They looked like friends," Grace repeated. "But I didn't stare. I tried to be discreet."

"Of course," Missy said. "It's not as if you could eavesdrop on the conversation."

"I wasn't close enough, which was a shame." She paused. "Though on my way to the ladies' room I did hear them discussing something that went on at school."

"I imagine Georgianna was tickled pink." Ella assumed the child had her hopes up for a happy ending. "I cannot imagine the two of them together, not after what her husband and his wife did."

"Well, that's water under the bridge now," Missy murmured.

Lou cleared her throat. "I have something—"

"Over the dam." Ella looked at the other women. "I thought it was 'water over the dam.'"

"Whatever," her sister said. "I have—"

"How about 'water over the bridge'?" Grace chuckled. "My mother used to say that. I suppose it doesn't make sense."

Lou stood up and waved her arms. "I have an announcement to make!"

"My goodness," Ella breathed, a little put out by such theatrics from her twin. "Why didn't you just *say* so?"

"You wouldn't let me, not with all that water talk."

"Do sit down, Lou, and try not to be so dramatic." Ella didn't like the sound of this, not one little bit. "You've been acting strangely for days."

"I'm moving in with Cameron," her sister announced.

"Why?" Ella asked, as the other two women

stared speechlessly at Louisa. "He lives next door. It's not as if he's in Barstow."

"We're going to live together," Lou said. "To see if we like it."

"Like *what?*"

Lou blushed. "Sex."

"Men always like sex," Ella declared. "It's eighty-year-old virgins who should have misgivings."

"Speak for yourself, dear," her sister said. "I'm moving out on New Year's Eve and I'm buying myself a black silk nightgown."

"It will never last," Ella said, trying to hide her dismay. What would she do in this big house by herself?

"My goodness," Missy said. "I don't know what to say."

Probably because she had the same gruesome picture in her head of Cameron and Louisa naked and in bed together, Ella decided. "I need a drink. Would anyone like wine or brandy?"

"Never mind the wine," Lou said. "I bought rum. Who wants a frozen strawberry margarita?"

"Lovely," said Grace.

"Good idea," Missy agreed.

"Make mine a double," Ella declared. "If I have to spend the rest of my life being nice to your live-in boyfriend, I might as well do it with a buzz on."

HE PLANNED to get over this infatuation with Maggie. If she was wearing a blue fuzzy sweater that matched her eyes and gave her the figure of Marilyn Monroe, so be it.

If she smiled at him across the school auditorium and he thought of escaping with her into the darkness of the parking lot and having his way with her against the cement wall of a public building, well, he would just have to get over it. Because he was a grown man who happened to have the hots for a woman he'd known almost all his life, a woman who was available—sort of—and who had told him it was too late.

Too late. What the hell did that mean? Gabe sat squashed into his seat and waited for the show to begin. His mother, busy talking to friends in the row in front of them, was seated beside him. His daughter was one of the sixth grade narrators, his son was a leaping lord. Behind him Calder and Lisette chatted with Mac, who was complaining that in his day they started shows on time and here it was twenty past seven already.

No, Gabe decided, glancing toward the middle row where Maggie sat with her mother and aunt. There was nothing he could do except be polite, if he could manage to ignore an erection the size of the Eiffel Tower. He rolled the construction paper program into a tube and wished they'd turn the lights off.

When the school principal, a tired-looking man in his forties, took the stage and asked everyone to welcome the kindergarten class on stage to sing "Jingle Bells," Gabe was only too happy for the show to begin.

"Lovely," his mother said seventy-seven minutes later, after the audience had joined together to sing "Silent Night."

"Yes. I'm glad you made it back in time."

"I couldn't stay in Tucson and miss the show," she said, taking her coat off the back of her chair. "The children would be so disappointed. Are we all set for tomorrow night?"

"Yeah. Kate's helping Maggie Moore with something in the afternoon, so I'll bring the kids to you when she's done."

"Good. I have lots to do," she said. His mother, an athletic woman with the energy level of a teenager, approached Christmas as if it was a shopping marathon. And she liked her grandchildren around to help her pick things out for them. A satisfactory arrangement all around, Gabe supposed.

"Good night, Gabe," Lisette called. "We'll see you tomorrow night."

"How lovely that you're getting out more," his

mother murmured. "Maybe you'll meet a nice woman like Calder did."

"Maybe." Maggie's daughters had joined her, he saw. She wore gray slacks, and when she bent over to give Lanie a hug, Gabe noticed how well those slacks hugged her very appealing ass.

"Is that Maggie Moore over there?" his mother asked.

"Yes."

"I haven't seen her in years, not since—"

"The funerals," Gabe finished for her. His mother had gone to Jeff's, too, out of respect for Jeff's mother, whom she'd grown up with. And she'd always had a soft spot in her heart for Maggie, though she'd referred to her as a "scamp" when she was young.

"She hasn't changed a bit."

"No?" He thought she looked different. In a good way.

"I'd like to say hello to Nona and Agnes," his mother insisted, poking him in the chest with her finger so he would move out of the aisle and let her get past him. "You could come with me."

"I could," he agreed, looking for Kate and Joe, who were nowhere to be seen. He would, too, if only to show Maggie that he could talk to her without grabbing her.

Her smile was a little uncertain when he approached, though she greeted his mother warmly. Neither he nor Maggie mentioned having dinner together last night, not that there was much to talk about. The four kids had done most of the talking, with Georgie and Joe telling stories about what went on at rehearsals and promising to behave themselves in the future. He and Maggie hadn't said more than three sentences to each other the whole time.

"I thought I'd come by and pick up the truck tomorrow," he told her. "Unless you've changed your mind."

"No. The Toyota seems to be okay."

"What time?"

"Morning would be best, though really anytime is fine, even if I'm not home."

He wanted her to be home. "All right. I'll have Hank drop me off. Have you come up with a price for cleaning out the sheds?"

"Yes, but when I do it depends on the weather."

So now they were going to talk about the weather. He figured he'd hit a new low. Meanwhile his mother was jabbering happily with Maggie's family, then asking Maggie about her antiques business.

"I hear primitive country chic is very fashionable right now," he heard his mother say. "I'd love to see your shop."

"I'm actually closed from December till April,"

Maggie said, "but you're welcome to come by anytime." She must have noticed Gabe's surprised look, because she explained that most of her business was on the Internet during the winter.

When his kids came running up, Gabe turned his attention to them and heard all about the twelve days of Christmas from a leaping lord's point of view. By the time Joe took a breath and Gabe could turn to Maggie, she was gone.

But he would see her in the morning. If he timed it just right, the kids would have gotten on the bus and Maggie would still be wearing her blue robe. It would be a test of his willpower, but he figured he was up to it.

MAGGIE DRESSED at dawn. There was no way Gabe O'Connor was going to surprise her again first thing in the morning. He didn't have to come inside to pick up his truck. In fact, chances were he wouldn't even so much as honk the horn as he drove out of the driveway.

But he'd asked if she'd be home. So that could mean he would come in again. And she was darn well going to be ready, with a clean kitchen and a fresh pot of coffee and absolutely no packing boxes stacked in corners.

She'd put the kids on the bus, walked along the snow-crusted driveway and, once inside, exchanged her waterproof boots for sheepskin slippers. She wore her oldest jeans and her favorite sweater, a white cashmere turtleneck she'd bought for seven dollars at the Salvation Army store two years ago but thought looked good. She put on lipstick and eyeliner and fixed her hair three different ways before letting it hang loose. She hoped it made her look more sophisticated, in a natural nonchalant kind of way.

She didn't want to be in love with Gabe again, Maggie decided, pouring herself a fresh cup of coffee. She'd gotten over her crush on the man the instant she heard he got married. That kind of news certainly destroyed all hope that Gabe would ever notice her *that* way. So when she heard his knock on the door and saw him standing on her porch, Maggie refused to let her heart beat faster. She opened the door and ushered him inside as if he stopped by for coffee every morning.

"I've grown up," she said, not realizing she'd spoken out loud until she saw the startled expression on his face.

"Yes," he said. "We both have. And I did not come here to make love to you."

"Well, that's good to know, but it wasn't exactly on my mind." Maggie set her coffee cup on the counter. She was such a liar. "I'd offer you coffee but I imagine you have a lot to do this morning."

"Coffee would be fine."

"Okay." She found her smallest coffee cup and filled it, then took it to the kitchen table. "You can sit down, Gabe."

"You're not wearing your blue robe." He sounded disappointed.

"I didn't want to inspire lust."

"Good decision." He smiled before sitting carefully on the wrought-iron chair. "It's bad enough without you walking around in your nightgown."

"What's bad enough?"

He took a sip of his coffee and set down the cup. "Wanting you. I think it was that red suit you wore to the wedding."

"Or maybe it was the champagne you drank."

"That, too," he conceded. "Or the fact that you danced with me and we'd never danced together before. It changed things somehow."

"Do you want every woman you dance with?" She knew she was flirting shamelessly, but this really was better than checking her eBay sales on the computer or painting thirty sap buckets sage green.

"I hadn't danced in a long time. Had you?"

"No." She sat near him, her coffee forgotten on the counter.

"You look good in blue, too." He eyed her sweater. "And white."

"Thank you." She wondered what he'd think of

her new velvet dress. Lisette said the outfit would torture the man and made it sound fun. "Wait until you see me in black."

"Black?"

"Tonight's dinner party," she reminded him.

"God, it's hot in here," he muttered, and unbuttoned his jacket.

"I have the woodstove going in the living room."

"Yeah, I can tell."

"So," she said, wondering what on earth they were doing talking about the temperature. "You've come for the truck."

"Since you insist, yes."

"I do."

"You always were too damn independent," Gabe said, though he looked at her as if he was thinking about something other than trucks. "Are you buying the Toyota?"

"Probably. It's more than I was prepared to spend, but Rob says it has lots of miles left."

"Gladding looks like a crook. Are you going to go out with him?"

She couldn't help but laugh. "That's none of your business."

"It feels like it is." He leaned forward and took her left hand. "You don't wear your wedding ring."

"Neither do you."

"I guess I stopped feeling married a long time

ago." He turned her hand over to look at her palm. "Green paint?"

"I was moving paint cans this morning."

He brought her fingers to his lips. "I promised myself I was going to keep my hands off you."

"You're flirting," she said. "You've never flirted with me before."

"Big mistake on my part." He curled her hand into a fist and rubbed her knuckles with his thumb. "I wasn't too smart when I was young."

"That's true." She thought about taking her hand away, but Gabe's touch was too good to resist. Maggie thought she should have more willpower.

"You said it was too late. You sure I can't change your mind?"

Willpower was vastly overrated, she decided. Even if she'd adored him when she was a kid, had a crush when she was in high school, fallen in love with him enough so that she thought it was the end of the world when he married someone else, and even if she might still be a little bit in love with him now, when he held her hand and told her she looked good in blue, was that any reason to wish he would lead her upstairs to bed and make love to her until lunchtime?

"Not exactly," Maggie said, wishing she'd worn the blue robe. "But I sure don't mind hearing you beg."

He laughed and tugged her toward him. "Kiss me, Maggie."

"Why?"

"Because you want to, of course." His lips were very close. "And because you feel sorry for me."

"I don't," she told him, "feel sorry for you."

"No?" He kissed her, a soft, exploring question that made her lean closer to him, so close she almost toppled from her chair.

"Are we supposed to know if this makes sense?"

"I don't think we care," he said.

"Okay." That sounded good to her. Not caring or worrying or thinking too hard. Only feeling Gabe's fingers on her skin and his mouth against hers and touching his cold jacket on the way to his throat. It was lovely to be kissed, to be lifted onto his lap, to wrap her arms around his neck and dissolve into the kind of kisses that until now she hadn't known existed in real life.

He still wore his jacket when he stood, holding her securely in his arms, and headed for the stairs. She was surprised for a second, then remembered he had been here a few times when he was a boy, when he or Owen or Cal would come to help her father with the haying or deliver a heifer or two.

"Upstairs?" Gabe asked.

"Good idea." Or she would most likely die of disappointment.

He carried her easily, which was impressive. And when he hesitated in the hall, she pointed toward her bedroom. Her childhood bedroom. She'd redone the large master bedroom for her daughters to share after Jeff died. She'd sold the bed and cleaned up her grandmother's iron headboard and washed an old yellow butterfly quilt she'd found on eBay.

And now Gabe was here with her, in the room with the windows that overlooked the backyard and the clothesline and the north pasture that had been sold thirty years ago to pay taxes.

"I'm really glad you're here," she told him. "But are you ever going to take your coat off?"

He set her on the bed and dropped his jacket to the wooden floor. "Better?"

"Much."

He joined her on the bed, tumbled her backward and made her laugh as he leaned over her, his arms braced on either side of her head. "How come we never did this in high school?"

"Because I never wore red?" She reached for his belt and despite trembling fingers did a pretty good job of unbuckling it.

"Could be." He leaned back. "Maggie, you have to stop doing that or I'll embarrass myself."

"Okay. You can take my clothes off first." She betrayed herself with a shaky smile. "I can't believe I said that."

"You know," he murmured, slipping one warm hand under her sweater. "We could stop talking for a while."

She gasped when his hand slid over her breast and dipped inside her bra. "Good idea," she managed to reply. "I'm starting to get a little speechless, anyway."

"That's flattering," Gabe said, "but we haven't even done anything yet."

"If you'd come a little closer we could start."

"Shh," was Gabe's only response, except that his fingers moved lower, to the snap of her jeans.

And then Maggie couldn't think of anything to say, because as hard as she tried she couldn't remember the last time she'd made love. Somehow they managed to get their clothes off. Somehow Grandma Johnson's quilt landed on the floor, and the vintage cotton sheet lay bunched at the foot of the bed, and Gabe's incredible and naked body lay on top of hers, though he was careful not to put his entire weight on her.

And somehow Maggie managed not to feel embarrassed about Gabe's appreciation of her naked body, illuminated with all its faults in the weak morning light. He didn't seem to notice that she should lose ten pounds or start doing sit-ups. He was as aroused as she was—she could feel him hot and hard against her inner thigh—and yet he took his time touching her, kissing her body with an un-abashed pleasure that made Maggie want to weep.

And return the favor.

She scooted onto her side and he, after a surprised look, moved onto his so they faced each other. And she could look at him, touch the furry mat of hair that covered his broad chest and memorize the feel of him under her fingertips. He was all hard muscle and warm skin, the body of a man who worked hard and long. There was still a hint of tan line around his neck; the rest of him was several shades lighter and covered with a pelt of dark hair. She traced a two-inch scar above his heart.

"Barbed wire," he said. "A stupid accident." She leaned forward and dragged her lips along the puckered skin.

"The pinto mare?" She looked up and met his gaze. He nodded, but from the look he gave her it was clear he didn't want to talk about horses.

She would have moved her hand lower, to touch that part of him that was hard against her hip, but Gabe took her wrist.

"Not this time," he whispered, kissing the corner of her mouth. And then he tumbled her gently onto her back and moved over her body. He brushed the hair that had fallen over her eyes. "I think," he said, "I have to be inside you now or lose all self-control."

She smiled at his need for her and thought she

would remember this morning for the rest of her life, the December day that Gabe came to her bed. He fit himself between her thighs and, with one smooth motion, entered her. And filled her. And made her sigh with the absolute rightness of it all.

She caressed his shoulders, felt his arms tremble, planted kisses in the hollow of his neck. He moved slowly, withdrawing partially and then filling her again with steady and deep strokes. She hadn't expected him to want her like this, as if he couldn't be inside her deeply enough. He paused to catch his breath, to let her catch hers, and held her face between his callused fingers.

"Is it—all right for you?" He was serious, she realized, as if having him inside her wasn't taking her breath away, as if her body hadn't wanted to climax in the first seconds he entered her.

"It's perfect," she whispered, tilting her hips slightly to bring him closer. "Don't stop."

He didn't, not until long after the exquisite tension broke and she tightened and came around him as he thrust into her. She heard him groan, felt him expand and climax, moving deep within her until he slowed and was finished.

She hoped Gabe felt as good as she did.

10

LUST WAS an odd thing. Or a fact of life, a part of nature, propagating the species and all that. Gabe drove the unwanted truck home and parked it beside the tractor shed. What he felt for Maggie fell into the category of lust, all right.

He still wanted her.

He wished he was still in that old iron bed, with all his clothes on the floor and naked, beautiful, luscious Maggie underneath him, with her thighs open and her body slick and ready for him.

Gabe groaned out loud. He'd had no business going over to her house this morning. He'd known damn well that he had no willpower, that seeing Maggie was like waving a red flag in front of a horny bull. He'd always liked being around Maggie, only years ago she was one of the guys. Oh, she'd grown breasts and wore lipstick and dated a couple of idiots from town once in a while, but Gabe never really thought about Maggie as a woman. About Maggie in bed. By the time she'd married Jeff Moore, Gabe had been too busy trying to keep his own marriage together without wondering about someone else's.

And then, at that damn wedding, it was like a switch went off and there he was, admiring Maggie instead of avoiding her. Looking at Maggie and not thinking about her wife-stealing husband. He didn't know what had happened to him, but he hoped it would disappear as fast as it came. He wasn't real comfortable with wanting a woman so badly.

Making love to Maggie had been like nothing else in his experience with women. He'd been all too aware of being inside her, a perfect fit. She was a woman generous with her body and her mouth and her touch, a woman who behaved as if he was giving her an incredible gift.

It was not a gift. It was lust. Lust between two people who were tired of being alone and tired of sleeping in a cold bed with no other warm body to curl next to. So he couldn't keep his hands off her. It didn't mean anything except that Maggie was a good-looking woman, and he was a man who had been alone too long.

There couldn't possibly be any more to it than that.

AFTER MAKING LOVE with Gabe, Maggie decided that checking her eBay auctions paled in comparison. Just about anything did. She switched off her computer and contemplated a not-very-nice thought—why Carole had preferred Jeff's lovemaking instead of her husband's.

There really was no comparison, Maggie thought. And not for the first time in the two hours since Gabe dressed and left as if he'd been called to fight a forest fire. An out-of-control forest fire.

He'd given her a look she couldn't interpret, kissed her once—hard, with his lips closed—and got out of Dodge, as the saying went.

She'd been too sated and relaxed to trip him, climb on top of his prone body and demand to know what he was running away from exactly, but she wished she'd thought of trying. Instead she'd pulled the covers over her shoulder and drifted off to sleep. Orgasms made her sleepy, not that there'd been that many with Jeff, but she didn't want to think ill of the dead. He must have saved his best moves for his lover.

She was dressed and showered and ready for the kids when the school bus arrived. Kate was ready to help package up the last of the Internet orders, Georgie wanted to make instant chocolate pudding to take to her grandmother's and Lanie fell asleep in front of the television set.

"My grandma is coming to pick me up at five," Kate informed her. "Daddy's going out tonight."

"Yes, I know. To the Browns for dinner, right?"

She double-checked an invoice and thought about Gabe's scar and the lovely part of his body that had throbbed against her when she'd kissed his chest.

"Yep. You're going, too, aren't you?"

"I sure am. I even bought a new dress." Georgie looked up from the pudding bowl as if she didn't believe her ears.

"A *new* dress? Really new or new old?"

"Really new," Maggie announced. "Made of black velvet."

Kate made an ooh sound and Georgie demanded to see for herself.

"Okay, but wash your hands." There would be no pudding on her dress tonight unless she spilled it herself. Because tonight she was going to be a glamorous temptress in velvet, a hot Montana babe with vintage rhinestones and the afterglow of morning sex.

"YOU'RE GLOWING." Lisette studied Maggie's expression as she lifted a carrot stick to her lips.

"Thank you," she said, giving Lisette a little smile. "I know."

Lisette turned to look at Gabe, who did his best to look innocent, as if he wasn't listening to anything the women talked about. Oh, sure, Cal and Owen also watched their women while pretending to discuss how Seattle would do in the playoff game tomorrow. And which college bowl game would be the best one to watch.

"Nebraska," Gabe declared, realizing that Maggie was indeed glowing. He'd almost had heart failure when she'd come through the living room door. Gabe had never seen her in something so low-cut and sleek and soft looking, except maybe that robe.

She knew it, too. Her blue eyes sparkled when she greeted him. He knew he'd surprised Cal's wife when he'd bent to kiss Maggie's cheek. He thought he showed great restraint by not continuing the kiss down her neck, along her throat and into those tempting plump breasts partially exposed under a shiny necklace.

"Nah," said Owen. "The Colorado game's going to be better. They've got that quarterback—"

Gabe's attention drifted once again to Maggie, who was seated across from him on the brown leather couch. She finished chewing a carrot and wiped her fingers on a little paper napkin. The shiny things on the necklace looked like little balls strung together, and when she leaned over the necklace hovered above her lap.

It was driving him crazy.

"You look sick." Cal handed him another whiskey and water. He glanced at Maggie, who was deep in conversation with Lisette and Suzanne, then to Gabe. "What's going on?"

"Nothing."

"Yeah?"

"I can handle it," he assured his friend, and took a sip of the unwanted drink. He thought he would need a clear head to avoid looking like a moonstruck calf.

"She could have brought a date tonight," Cal said, settling himself into the chair beside him. "But she didn't."

"Wise of her. I would have had to kill him."

"So that's the way it is. Not just friends anymore?"

"I don't know." Which was the truth. He turned to Calder and saw that his friend wasn't laughing. "This is all pretty strange."

"No shit. Two months ago none of us was married, and now look at me and Chase." They both looked at Owen, who was leaning over to whisper something to his wife. Suzanne shook her head and laughed.

"I'm not looking to get married," Gabe said, keeping his voice low. He wasn't going to put himself through that nightmare again. Life with Carole had taught him some lessons he wouldn't soon forget. "Been there, done that. Not your typical happy ending."

"You were doomed from the start, pal. Carole

was high maintenance and low patience. Not your type."

"Yeah. I caught on." His type, Gabe decided, ran to voluptuous blondes with green paint on their fingers. Or more particularly, a ferociously independent woman who could use a decent truck and a new bed and a dress with a higher neckline.

"Well, Carole *was* a good-looking woman," Cal said. "It's not like your judgment was totally screwed up."

"Thanks." He kept his gaze on Maggie, who seemed relaxed and unaware that she was driving him crazy every time she leaned over to pick up something from the vegetable tray.

"You seem on track now, though."

"Yeah?" He took a healthy swallow of his drink as Maggie crunched another carrot stick. "How's that?"

"It's that pathetic look on your face. Women like that." Cal chuckled. "I'd better go refill your date's wineglass."

"She's not my date." They'd arrived in separate trucks, though he wished he'd thought to pick her up. "We didn't come here together."

"Your kids are with Grandma, right?"

"Yeah." The house had been completely, eerily silent while he was getting dressed. He'd plugged in the lights on the Christmas tree and sat in the living room all by himself to look at it and had felt a little strange.

"And Maggie's kids, I heard, are at *her* mother's house in town. So," Cal drawled, rattling the ice cubes in his almost empty glass. "Do you believe in fate?"

"I do now." Gabe smiled, and Maggie looked over and caught him. Her eyebrows rose as if to say, *What's so funny, pal?* He shrugged, then she surprised him and winked.

Fate, Gabe decided, had given him another chance with Maggie.

"YOU'VE SLEPT WITH HIM, haven't you?" Lisette handed her a large pottery bowl filled with tossed salad. It smelled heavenly, of garlic and basil.

"What kind of dressing is this?"

"A family secret, and don't change the subject." Lisette, in emerald satin slacks and matching tunic, followed her to the table set for six at one end of the massive Brown kitchen. Lisette had layered gold and red tablecloths, arranged fat red candles on silver dishes and polished the family silver; the effect was breathtaking.

"It's beautiful," Maggie told her. "All this and food, too?"

"Thank you. I love to entertain, and it's been so long since—" She frowned and shook her finger.

"Never mind that. Hurry, before the men come in, and tell me what's going on."

"Tell me, too," Suzanne said, entering the kitchen with a tray of empty glasses. "I'm starved for female companionship over the age of fourteen. By the way, Maggie, I love that dress."

"Thanks. It's my Christmas gift to myself."

Lisette peered down the empty hall. "Where are they?"

"They went in the office to look at something. Grass seed, I think," Suzanne said. "What's going on? Christmas present secrets?"

"Maggie bought that dress to drive Gabe crazy," Lisette explained. "We think it's working."

"I noticed he can't take his eyes off you."

"I've known that man all my life," Maggie said. "And he came over to my house this morning and we ended up in bed."

The two women stared at her. Lisette's mouth dropped open, but no words came out right away.

"You didn't need that dress at all," she said finally.

"I'm not sure what happened. It just seemed...right." She felt her cheeks grow warm. "It was. Right, I mean."

"Well, congratulations," Suzanne told her. "Owen and I were stranded in a snowstorm at his ranch the first time. It was perfect. I missed my plane."

They looked at Lisette, who reached for her half-empty wineglass and polished off the rest of her Pinot Grigio. "Oh, all right. I'll tell. The table," she said, almost whispering. "I came here to cater a party and I ended up under that—" she pointed to the beautifully decorated dining room table "—with Calder."

"All of a sudden my morning's starting to feel pretty tame," Maggie declared.

"Oh, damn," Suzanne said. "Here come the men."

"We must pretend we were talking about food," Lisette said, and they laughed. And when Lisette seated them, Gabe was next to Maggie, on her left, as if they were already a couple. And if his hand grazed her thigh or she leaned close to him in order to hear something Cal was saying about his new daughters' Christmas gifts, no one was surprised. Owen may have smiled and Calder may have winked, but the women pretended everything was going according to plan. Though Maggie didn't have a *real* plan, except to enjoy herself.

That was enough.

For now.

"FOREPLAY," Gabe announced, as if he'd invented it.

"Excuse me?" Maggie checked to make sure her dress was out of the way before she shut the truck door. She had known he would follow her home, had taken great pleasure in the headlights behind her on the empty road, knowing that Gabe was there.

"That whole evening, from start to finish," he said, striding toward her. "Was foreplay, pure and simple."

"Is that a complaint?" Maggie wanted to laugh at the power of velvet and rhinestones.

"Not exactly." She could see his breath in the cold air. "Though I didn't get to finish dessert."

"You don't like cream puffs?"

"I love them. But you had your hand on my thigh." He took her hand and turned it over, palm up, and studied it. "Hey," he said. "No paint."

"I will never put my hand on your thigh again," she promised. "Unless your leg is pressing against mine under the table."

"I couldn't help myself," he explained, looking at her with laughing eyes. "Your breasts were falling out of your dress."

"It's called cleavage, cowboy."

"It's called torture, sweetheart." He smiled and kept hold of her hand. "Are you going to invite me in?"

"If you like."

"I'd *like* to undress you," Gabe murmured. "Though not right away."

She led him toward the door where a light shone on the back porch steps. "You'd like coffee first?"

"Hell, no."

Maggie took her hand from his and fumbled through her purse for her key chain. "Beer, wine, whiskey, brandy, cigars, the sports report on CNN?"

"It's a good thing I'm not paying attention to you," he said. He lifted her hair and placed a kiss on the back of her neck, above the collar of her coat. It gave her goose bumps and made her think of things to come. She sighed and turned the key in the lock.

"It's a good thing we're all alone," she replied, reluctant to switch on the overhead light. Gabe shut the door behind him, then enfolded her in his arms and tucked her against his body. She could feel the warm length of him on her back, his breath tickling her neck. "We can talk about foreplay now."

"Talk?" he asked, unbuttoning her coat with surprising ease. "Or do?"

"You decide."

He turned her so she faced him. "I think," he said slowly, "you have tortured me enough for one night. Now it's my turn."

Her body responded with delicious heat in all the right places. "Oh, good."

This time he knew the way to her bedroom. She'd left a light on in the upstairs hall, which showed the way. Gabe didn't let go of her hand until they were near her bed, and then only to remove her jacket from her shoulders and toss it aside.

"I like that dress," he murmured, standing back a little to admire her.

"You're embarrassing me." She managed to kick off her boots.

"I don't mean to. Don't you know how beautiful you look?"

She smiled. "I hoped you'd think so."

"Turn around." Maggie did, leaving Gabe free to unzip the back of the dress just enough to ease the velvet from her shoulders. His fingers slipped under her hair and lower, to skim over her breasts and drop the velvet that barely covered them. When his hands cupped her breasts and tested their weight, Maggie wondered how much longer she would be able to stand. She felt warm and languorous, sultry and inexperienced, shy and yet very aroused. He had a way of touching her that made her wonder at her reaction.

"I've wanted to do this all night," he said, his voice low and raspy, as if he, too, was affected.

"Foreplay," she whispered.

"Definitely. Tell me," he said, into her ear. "We have all night?"

"Yes."

"Tell me what you like," he said, thumbing her nipples into tight peaks. "Tell me how you like to be touched and held and made love to."

"This is a very good start," she managed to say, though she closed her eyes and leaned her head back against his shoulder. Her skin was on fire, the rhinestones cold as they shifted across her breasts.

He undressed her, slowly and with kisses. The silk garter belt and black stockings she'd found in a box lot of linens at an auction last summer made Gabe draw in his breath. She'd hoped he would re-act with pleasure, but she didn't expect him to become totally speechless.

"I have a secret passion for vintage clothing," she explained, but Gabe sat on the edge of the bed, at eye level with her belly button and inches from the scraps of lace that covered her, and said nothing.

"I think the stockings are from the thirties," she explained. "They were in an elegant pink cardboard box, as if they'd never been worn."

The man was silent still.

"I like to go to auctions," Maggie continued, tempted to rap him on the top of his head, just in case he had gone into a coma or something. "I never know what I'm going to find."

Not a sound, as if he held his breath.

She settled for tugging a fistful of his hair. "Hey, pal, are you asleep or what?"

Gabe leaned forward and, holding her hips, ran his tongue along the silk-covered elastic. "I'm not asleep," he said, moving lower. "I'm in shock."

"Good." She sighed with the absolute pleasure of it all. Her body was positively humming. And the night had barely begun. Gabe skimmed kisses along the silk, slipped her bikini underwear down her thighs, found her with his tongue and brought her so close to climaxing that she cried out with desire. He unhooked the stockings, slipped his finger in the elastic of the garter and dragged it down her hips.

"I think," he said, dropping the bits of silk at her ankles, "that Christmas has come a few days early."

"Ho, ho, ho." It was the last thing Maggie was able to say coherently for a long, long time, because Gabe pulled her closer to his mouth and pleasured her until she came against his tongue. He lifted her onto the bed, removed his clothes and lay back against the mound of pillows to catch his breath. He could taste her on his lips, in his mouth, and he was hard with desire.

"Come here," he said, guiding her over him. The rhinestones dangled low, past her breasts. And when she leaned forward to kiss his mouth her breasts swept his chest, and so did the necklace. He saw the uncertainty on her face when he lifted her hips and guided himself into her. She was wet and slick, ready for him and yet so sweetly tight around him.

"Oh," she said, a soft little sound of surprise, of what he hoped was satisfaction. He moved inside her, urged her into a rhythm that took him deep inside her. Gabe didn't know how long they made love to each other that way, but he knew that for the rest of his life he would remember this. Maggie leaned forward and found his mouth right before she tightened and came. His large hands cupped her buttocks as he came inside her, hard and fast and long. And later, much later, when they both caught their breath, Gabe realized that they were not going to stop making love until sunrise.

She was still on top of him when he touched the rope of beads splayed against his collarbone. "What is this exactly?"

"A very old necklace my aunt gave me. It supposedly belonged to a woman who ran a brothel in Idaho."

"You like old things," he murmured, rubbing one of the balls between his thumb and forefinger.

"Yes. Especially this," Maggie said. "I think it brought me good luck. After all, there's a naked man in my bed."

"Is that all you need to make you feel lucky?"

"I could also win the lottery. Buy myself a brand-new fancy pickup truck. Santa Claus could bring me a freezer full of chicken pot pies."

"Why chicken pot pies?"

"I'm a terrible cook," she confessed. "Lisette's offered to give me lessons."

"You have other talents," Gabe told her, tipping her onto her back and rolling on top of her. Too many talents to list, he thought, nestling his hardening penis between her soft thighs.

So many talents he hadn't appreciated until now. He'd been such a fool.

of the Horse Club, gazed back in the comfort of the

11

GABE WOKE at dawn Saturday, his usual time, and slipped from under the covers without disturbing the sleeping woman beside him. Maggie lay on her side, facing away from him, independent in sleep as she was awake. He retrieved his clothes and, boots in hand, tiptoed out of the room and down the stairs. There was work to do at home; the children wouldn't return until lunchtime, and Gabe had some thinking to do.

He wasn't sure how or when he'd fallen in love with Maggie, but he knew his life had changed in the past twenty-four hours. Even if he wasn't sure what to do about it. He didn't like to rush into things, but then again, there were other men waiting in the wings, like the skinny veterinarian and the sleazy truck salesman. Neither of them deserved Maggie and her auction underwear, her funny children or her love. He wasn't sure she loved him, either, but he figured he had a shot at it.

If he played his cards right.

MAC, special invited guest at the weekly breakfast of the Hearts Club, leaned back in the corner of the booth and, over the background noise of the bowling alley, proved he was worthy of free pancakes and eggs. Courtesy of Ella, of course, who'd asked him to come.

"Now this is just from Calder," Mac drawled. "We were both up real early with Lisette, but she was too busy to have much to say."

The four women nodded. They knew what life was like with Christmas arriving the day after tomorrow.

"This is the longest time I'll sit down for the next three days," Grace declared. "The kids start coming home this afternoon."

"Well, it's nice to have company," the old rancher said. "I sure like having children in the house again, though I'm thinking I ought to find me a new place to live and leave the big house to the young folks."

Ella swore her blood turned cold. She picked up her coffee cup with shaking fingers and hoped no one noticed. She certainly hoped Mac wasn't hinting that he'd like to move to town. To her street. To her *house*, as if this "living together" idea was contagious. One Bliss sister living in sin was quite enough, thank you, though Louisa hadn't moved out yet or bought her fancy black nightgown.

"Please, Mac," Louisa said. "Tell us all about the party. What did Lisette make for dinner?"

"We didn't ask Mac here to talk about food." Ella set her cup on the table a little harder than she intended, and coffee sloshed over the brim. "We want to know how it went with Gabe and Maggie."

"Oh, it went, all right," Mac said. "I guess Maggie just about drove that poor young man crazy last night. Calder said she was all dressed up in something fancy that showed—well—" Mac stopped to gulp some coffee. "That, uh, showed how pretty she is."

"She is lovely," Missy agreed. "I think Dr. Hathaway was quite taken with her."

"Shh." Ella wanted to hear Mac's opinion. "What else?"

"I guess Lisette made sure they sat together. Calder figures there was some hanky-panky goin' on under the table because Maggie kept blushing and looking happy."

"What kind of hanky-panky?" Louisa leaned forward, obviously wanting more information for her sexual repertoire.

"Lou, hon, I just wouldn't know." Mac shook his head. "I can't say I'm much of an expert on dinner parties and such behavior. I'm just repeating what Calder said, and he was laughing pretty hard."

"Laughing?" Ella didn't know what was so humorous about this romance. Matchmaking was not to be taken lightly. "At Maggie?"

"No, Ella." He took another sip of coffee. "Not laughing at Maggie. At Gabe, for finally getting bit by the love bug, so to speak."

"I guess that's that," Ella said. "I wonder if Georgie is aware that she is about to get the stepfather she wants."

"Will you call her?" The question came from Missy, who had a soft spot in her heart for children of any age.

"No. Not now. Plenty of time to celebrate *after* they're married."

"Married?"

"What?" Ella asked, surprised at Mac's question. "Isn't that what we're all working for here?"

"I dunno." The man shrugged. "I think you're getting a little ahead of yourself there, sweetheart."

Ella decided to let the sweetheart remark go without comment.

"And what about last night's dessert?" Grace asked. "What did Lisette make?"

"Cream puffs," he replied. "Only she has some fancy French name for them. Profit something."

"Profiteroles," Missy said, surprising them with her French accent that sounded rather uppity and smart. "That's what they call them in Paris."

"Yep." Mac nodded. "That's them, all right. Profeet-rolls." He winked at Ella. "We're learning lots of fancy new things out at the ranch. That's why I figure I'd better get out of there, before I lose all my down-home charm."

Fat chance of that, Ella thought, looking away from him and stabbing the last piece of French toast with her fork. Charm might ooze out of Robert MacKenzie Brown's every pore, but she could deal with him.

From a comfortable distance.

NO ONE at the post office was happy to see Maggie Moore arrive. She and Aunt Nona made three trips to bring all her packages inside, and the folks that arrived after her knew they were going to spend more time than they'd planned in the post office.

"Well, young lady, you're certainly cheerful this morning. Your date go well?" No one could ever put anything over on Nona.

"I have Christmas spirit," Maggie explained. *I had Gabe O'Connor in my bed all night.*

"Ha." Nona snorted, ignoring the looks of the other people in line for the postmaster. Today her aunt wore a vintage wool coat with a soft brown mink collar over a long suede skirt and high-heeled boots. "You've got more than Christmas spirit, my darling. You have that look in your eyes."

"What look?"

"That 'I have a man' look."

Oh, dear. Maggie looked away, hoping to erase any messages her eyes were giving. "I wonder if the snow will hold off for another day."

"You're a funny one," Nona said. "You've been in love with that man forever and thought no one noticed."

"Not forever," Maggie countered, wishing Nona would lower her voice. "And maybe not even now."

"You can't fool me." Nona helped her shove the pile of boxes closer to the counter as the line moved forward. "I just hope you get out more, like you did last night. Agnes and I sure enjoy having those kids over. Especially Agnes. She loves those girls, probably reminds her of raising you. I think she misses the ranch more than she lets on. What time do you want us to bring the turkey Monday?"

"Any time," Maggie said, trying to keep up with the fast pace of the conversation. She didn't think she'd had much sleep last night, and she was still groggy from sleeping late. "You know, you could spend the night Christmas Eve, if you want. We could cook the bird in my oven."

"We both like our own beds," Nona said. "You know that. Besides, you have enough to do with the children without dealing with company, too."

He'd left before she was awake, which was just as

well, Maggie had decided. He would have work to do, his children to retrieve, Christmas errands and all sorts of things to accomplish the day before Christmas Eve. She wondered what he would be doing for Christmas. Dinner with his mother on the ranch, she supposed. Or maybe with Cal and Lisette.

"Maggie," Nona said. "Move it!"

"Sorry." She tried to concentrate on the job at hand, lifting the packages to be mailed to the high bidders of her eBay auctions. Business had been especially good this month, despite the expected holiday drop. "Remember that antique saddle I won at the church potluck supper?"

"You put it up for sale? Good for you." Nona greeted the postmaster, a weary-looking woman who managed to smile and wish them a merry Christmas as they stacked boxes on the counter.

"Merry Christmas," Maggie replied. "I promise, Betty, this is the last batch for the next five or six days." She turned to Nona. "I listed it with a high reserve, so if it doesn't meet the price I'll relist it and try again. The auction ends tonight."

"The person who buys that is going to have one heck of a shipping bill," her aunt said.

"That's the drawback," Maggie said, pulling her checkbook out of her purse. "I can't wait to see what happens tonight."

"No date? No dinner party? No evening with you-know-who?"

"The dress was a hit, the necklace—" oh, how she remembered wearing the necklace while making love with Gabe "—was lovely and sparkly, but—"

"There's a but to this?" Nona looked amused.

"But I intend to work tonight. And wrap presents. And try to make cookies." At this announcement her aunt rolled her eyes. "I don't have time for, um, you-know-who."

But, Maggie thought, the you-know-what was certainly more exciting than sitting at her computer. And she continued to think so, long hours later when the girls were finally in bed and the only thrill came from selling the saddle for enough money for a down payment on Rob Gladding's truck.

"WE'RE GOIN' OVER to Georgie's house tonight," Joey announced. Gabe looked up from his breakfast of steak and eggs.

"We are?" He didn't remember Maggie saying anything about getting together on Christmas Eve. He should have called her yesterday, but he'd wanted to—well, he'd figured they both could use some time to get used to the idea of each other.

Or something like that. He'd wanted to see her today. Wanted to see her every day.

"Yep." His son grinned. "Cool, huh?"

"And how do you know this is what we're doing? Did Maggie—Mrs. Moore—call while I was outside?"

Joey shrugged. "I dunno. I just know we hafta be there at five o'clock. They're decoratin' their tree."

"Maybe they need help," Gabe said, thinking this sounded pretty good. He'd wondered how to see her, wanted to talk to her about her plans for Christmas, when he should call. He figured he would have run into her in town today, but all he'd seen was the Toyota parked at her aunt's house. She would have been picking up her kids, just like he was picking up his. "Five o'clock, you said?"

Joey nodded. "Yep."

"All right. I'll call her, find out if we can bring anything."

"They're not home," his son said. "They're, uh, at their grandma's all day."

Gabe wondered if he should bring a bottle of wine. If Maggie would wear her blue sweater, if she would smile at him as if she was glad to see him. He wouldn't kiss her in front of the children, though he would touch her back with his fingers, feel the warmth of her under his hand. It would have to be enough until they could be alone again.

"Dad?"

"Hmm?"

"Georgie says Lanie still believes in Santa, so don't say anything."

"No problem. I'll be careful."

"Dad?"

"Yeah?"

Joey hung on Gabe's chair and leaned his head on his shoulder. "What do you want for Christmas?"

"Candy canes, socks, maybe a new flashlight." *Maggie. Just Maggie.*

"SOMEONE'S HERE," Georgie announced, peering through the door's window. "I see headlights."

"I'm not expecting anyone," Maggie said, stepping into the kitchen. She should never, ever have tried putting up the Christmas tree on Christmas Eve again. Just because Jeff's parents did it that way and he'd insisted it wouldn't be Christmas if the tree wasn't fresh and that is what Georgie expected—

"Mom! It's Mr. O'Connor!"

"It is?" She attempted to pull her hair back, but her fingers had sap on them, and the hair stuck, making it worse. She wore her oldest jeans and her ugliest boots; there were pine needles stuck in her sweater and an unpleasant odor coming from the oven. "Georgie, is the pizza burning?"

"Nope. It's not in yet."

"Oh, good heavens." She should have cleaned her oven after the sweet potatoes exploded on

Thanksgiving. What was Gabe doing here, anyway? Maggie told herself she wasn't hurt that he didn't call her yesterday, just to make sure she hadn't died in her sleep. And now she was a mess, not a sultry temptress in rhinestones or wearing her movie-star robe.

Life wasn't at all fair.

Georgie, of course, eagerly opened the door, letting in a gust of welcome fresh air. "Hi!"

"Merry Christmas," Gabe said, ushering Kate and Joey into the kitchen while Maggie stood there and gaped at him. The man carried a bottle of wine with a red bow tied around its neck, and Kate set a platter of cookies on the kitchen table.

"Merry Christmas," Maggie managed to say, only because she couldn't think of anything else. He looked incredibly handsome, incredibly clean, and the last time she'd seen him he'd kissed her before she fell asleep.

"This is so cool," Georgie said, grinning at Joe and Kate. "Want to see our tree? Lanie's getting the ornaments ready, and Mom was fixing the lights." They scrambled through the door into the living room and disappeared.

"Well," she said, trying to wipe the sap off her fingers by rubbing them on her jeans. "This is a surprise."

"Yeah." He smiled. "Four kids and we're alone in the kitchen."

"I meant that you're here. I'm glad to see you, but I would have cleaned up the house and—"

"You invited us," Gabe said, looking at her as if she'd lost her mind. "To help put up your tree. I have a saw in the truck, just in case—"

"I did?"

"Joey said—" And then Gabe stopped and laughed. "I think my son set me up, probably because he wanted to come over here and be with Georgie."

"And Georgie probably helped him come up with the idea." She turned and stuck her head into the living room. "Georgie, come here for a minute." Gabe came up behind her and motioned to Joey, whose expression of guilt was almost comical.

"What's that smell?"

Maggie sniffed. And coughed. And didn't think at all of sweet potatoes. "It smells like—"

"Do you have a cat?"

"No." But the unmistakable smell in the room was exactly like a wet diaper or the inside of a bathroom that needed to be cleaned. "I don't know—"

"A dog? A ferret?" He sniffed again and walked into the living room. Maggie winced when she saw the room through company's eyes. The woodstove cheerfully blasted heat from its corner hearth, but she hadn't had time to sweep the bits of bark from the bricks. The carpet needed to be vacuumed, but she'd intended to do that later, after the tree was decorated and the boxes put away. Ornaments and tissue paper lay scattered everywhere, as Lanie's idea of unpacking was to lay ornaments on every available surface.

And the tree—well, the tree sat in its stand waiting for lights.

"The tree stinks," Joe announced.

"Pee," Lanie said, crinkling her nose. "Yuk."

Kate's eyes were huge as she turned and looked at her father. "Daddy?"

He cleared his throat. "Maggie, where did you get it?"

"I bought it from that place outside of town last week. I took it home and leaned it up against the shed until tonight."

"Well," he said, going closer to the damn tree than Maggie thought was necessary. And then compounding her embarrassment by sniffing it, he added, "I'll bet that a stray dog or cat was, ah, using it while you had it outside. You'd have seen the yellow snow in the daylight, I'll bet." When he turned to look at her, Maggie could tell he didn't know whether to laugh or feel sorry for her. "I'll get it out of here for you."

"Thanks. I'll open some windows and see—"

"You're taking our tree?" Georgie asked, her voice a little shrill. "Then we won't have a tree for Christmas!"

"We can't have a tree that smells like dog pee," Maggie said. "The whole house is going to smell bad."

"But what are we going to do?"

"You can have ours," Joey said, surprising everyone.

"Oh, Joey, that's really sweet," Maggie told him. "But we can't take your tree."

"Then you could come to our house and *look* at it," the boy insisted, looking very much like his father. Maggie threw her arm over his shoulders and hugged him to her.

"We'll get another tree," she said. "It's not too late."

"It's not?" Lanie sniffed, tears welling in her eyes. "Really, Mom?"

She glanced at her watch. Surely something would still be open. "The gas station sells trees. They wouldn't be closed this early."

"I'll go," Gabe offered. She realized he'd never even taken his jacket off. She was a terrible hostess. Her house smelled like a kennel, she smelled like pine sap, the house was a mess, and there was nothing to offer the O'Connors except frozen pizza. *Cheap* frozen pizza.

"But I get to pick it out," Lanie said. "It's my turn."

"Lanie—"

"She can go with me," Gabe offered. "You all can. I have the Suburban, so there's plenty of room."

"I'll stay here," she said. "I'll, um, get the lights untangled." She would change her clothes, find some air freshener to spray, open all the windows and put on some lipstick.

"I can help," Kate offered, with a wide-eyed look at the messy kitchen.

"Sure," Maggie told her, then turned to Gabe, who had reached in with one hand and grabbed the tree by its trunk, lifting it easily. With the other he removed the stand from the tree's base. "We'll toss some frozen pizzas in the oven when you come back."

"I'll bring some food back with me," he said. "It'll come out of Joey's allowance. Since he planned this party, he can pay for it."

"Georgie will help," Maggie said, giving her daughter a stern look. "I don't think Joey thought this up all by himself."

The little girl headed for the stairs. "I'll get my money. Don't leave without me!"

Gabe promised he wouldn't, told Joey to open the door for him and then tossed her stinky Christmas tree out into the night. Lanie burst into tears and sobbed that Santa Claus was never going to come to her house now.

If Maggie had planned a second date, this would not have been it.

So it shouldn't have come as a big surprise when Gabe and the children returned with half a tree—deformed, but with the appropriate scent—and with two bags of potato chips, three bottles of cola and a package of candy canes.

"Nothing was open except the gas station," Gabe explained. "And this was the last tree."

He didn't look as cheerful or as in charge as he had when he'd left the house, Maggie noticed. By the time they'd brought the tree into the living room and fixed it in the stand, the bottoms of the pizzas had burned, Maggie's mother had called twice—once to check on the time for tomorrow's dinner and then again to ask if the girls minded celery in the stuffing—and Joe flopped on the couch complaining of a stomach ache.

Maggie figured he needed some fresh air, since it was going to take longer than she thought to get rid of the dog pee smell, and told him to sit in front of an opened window.

Two strings of lights didn't work, another was stepped on, and the long strand of vintage silver tinsel that Maggie thought was so elegant when she'd discovered it at a yard sale, looked as if it had barely survived the *Titanic*. Joe revived, and somehow the children managed to decorate the tree, making it look festive and cheerful. Maggie served pizza and cola, which they ate in the living room while they hung ornaments. And Gabe didn't have much to say. Oh, he hung the battered gold star on the top of the tree and he lifted Lanie so she could hang ornaments on the high branches, but he didn't have any pizza. And the wine bottle sat unopened on the kitchen counter, though the cookies disappeared quickly when Kate fetched them from the table.

Maggie figured he'd had enough when he stood and told his children it was time to go home.

"It's only seven-thirty," Kate said, disappointed.

"Yeah, Dad," Joey added. "It's early."

"Santa's going to come," Lanie said. "Tonight."

"Which is why we need to go home," Gabe told her. "Come on, kids, get your coats and thank Mrs. Moore for the pizza. And Joe? You have an apology to make."

"I'm sorry we tricked you," the boy said, looking anything but sorry. "But we had fun."

"Yes," Maggie said. From a child's point of view, pizza, cookies, cola and tree-decorating added up to a pretty good time. She looked at Gabe, whose expression was almost stern.

"Not the kind of evening you pictured, huh, O'Connor?" She tried for a light tone, hoping to make him smile. "No perfect tree, elegant meal, children singing 'Silent Night'?"

He frowned. "What?"

"No rhinestones, no velvet, no champagne."

"Not exactly. You know," he said, dropping his voice low. "I'd thought tonight would be my big chance. I'd ask you to get married, make a big romantic proposal, the whole thing."

Her heart lifted, soared, plummeted to her ugly boots. "But you're not going to," she said, wondering if she had actually heard correctly.

"Hell, no, Maggie," he muttered, jamming his Stetson on top of his dark hair. "Not *now*."

Beside her Joe made a noise and ran after Georgie, who screeched in delight. Lanie started to cry again—something about Santa not liking the way the house smelled—and then Gabe turned to gather up his two kids.

Maggie stood unmoving, conscious of the complete chaos of her house. Well, he'd gotten a glimpse of the World According to Moore, enough to kill passion in a lesser man.

And she wouldn't have said yes anyway.

12

"ELLA, DO SIT DOWN, DEAR. What on earth is the matter with you tonight?"

Ella looked at her sister and sighed. "I suppose I'm experiencing some holiday stress."

"Stress?" Louisa poured cognac into two liqueur glasses and handed Ella one. "Whatever are you stressed about?"

"For one thing, you're moving, Lou. I don't do well with change." To say nothing of the fact that Mac was on his way over, having invited himself to the house for a Christmas Eve nightcap.

Louisa sank into the wing chair and took a sip of her drink. "I will be living right next door. Not that far away at all."

"I realize that." Ella sighed, looking at the artificial Christmas tree Cam and Lou had erected last week. Louisa insisted upon putting it in front of the window that faced Elm Street, so the lights would look festive to everyone who drove by. "Mac should be here any minute now."

"A gentleman caller." They both looked at the

portrait of their father that hung over the mantel. "Father never approved of any of our gentlemen callers, did he?"

"He didn't want us to leave him," Ella said, wondering at the tears that threatened to fill her old, tired eyes. "I suppose I'm behaving the same way, not wanting you to leave me. It isn't very nice, is it."

"No." But Lou chuckled, her double chins shaking with good humor. "But understandable, because I am *such* good company."

"Oh, stop your nonsense," Ella said, at the same time the doorbell rang, announcing Mac's arrival.

"My, my," Lou said. She always made a huge event out of opening a gift. "What could it be?"

"Since your boyfriend has been and gone, it must be that old fool rancher," Ella said, opening the front door. "Oh, Mac, what on earth?"

Standing in front of her, then quickly ushered into her living room, were Georgianna Moore and, if Ella remembered correctly, the little O'Connor boy. Mac was red in the face and almost hyperventilating.

"Ella, my God, this is a new one!"

"Mac, you'd better sit down." She wondered if he was having a heart attack. She'd never seen the old rancher so upset. "Is it your heart, do you think?"

Lou hurried over and helped the children take their coats off. "My goodness," she clucked. "You two are out late on Christmas Eve. Have you been looking for Santa?"

"No, ma'am," Georgianna said. "We came to talk to you."

"To us?" Ella asked, looking at Mac, who shook his head and uttered something unintelligible under his breath. She decided she was fortunate not to hear it.

"I caught them riding their horses to town," Mac explained. When the Bliss sisters stared at him, he repeated, "They rode to town. *Rode,*" he repeated. "At night."

"Mac, dear, we understand." She motioned to Lou. "Louisa is going to pour you a nice stiff drink, and you are going to sit down."

"It's very important," the little girl added. "And we've been ridin' horses since we were three."

"Their parents—" Mac said, almost frantic. "We have to call—"

"Not yet, please," Georgianna said, as calm as a little adult. Ella was impressed. "I need to talk to Miss Ella."

"We need some advice," Joey declared. "It's kind of an emergency."

"An emergency?" Mac looked as if he wanted to throttle the child. "An emergency is when your house is on fire or your father is ill or you're being chased by bandits. Getting *advice* is not an emergency! You don't hop on a horse like you're in the middle of the back pasture and ride to town in the middle of the night in December!"

"Oh, my goodness," Lou breathed. She handed Mac a tiny glass filled with cognac, which he drank in one swallow, then handed the glass back to her. "No wonder you're upset."

"Lucky thing I saw them on the side of the road, almost had heart failure when I saw those two riding along the side of the road like it was a June afternoon. So I pulled over, hitched the horses to the back of my pickup and made the kids get in the cab with me. We went real slow, of course, for the horses' sakes."

"And your parents?" Ella said, leading them into the living room. She pointed to the sofa, where the two children sat down side by side. "I'm sure they're frantic with worry."

"The phone," Mac said, but Lou gave him another glass, this time a larger one filled with Father's best cognac, the bottle they used on special occasions, such as Christmas Eve. It was meant to be sipped, but Mac either didn't know or didn't care. He drank half of it in one gulp. At this rate she'd have a drunken rancher on her hands.

"In a minute," Ella said, turning to the children. "What sort of advice are you seeking?"

"Matchmaking, of course," Georgie replied, giving Ella a look that said, *What else?* "Mr. O'Connor came over tonight—Joey and I fixed it so he would, but we didn't get in much trouble—"

"You can't get in trouble on Christmas Eve," the boy interjected.

"But our tree smelled and we had chips and soda pop and then he said he was gonna ask Mom to marry him but he wasn't gonna do it."

"Changed his mind," Joey said.

"So now what?" Georgianna looked at her with big, sad, blue eyes. "I want a dad. Now."

"We don't always get what we want," Louisa told the children. Ella knew this was no time for molly-coddling, but if the children had come to them for help, well, all was not lost.

"It is simple enough to bring your parents together," she said, knowing she was the center of attention. She looked toward Mac. "Are you well enough to call Gabe and Maggie now?"

"Yep. I hope your daddy tans your hide, Christmas or no Christmas," Mac told Joey. "I'll have to tell him to hitch up his horse trailer, too, because I'm sure you ladies don't want horses on your front lawn all night."

"Mac," Ella warned. "Just make the call." She looked at the children, who had begun to look a little nervous. "Of course, your mother and your father must decide—all by themselves—if they want to marry or not. But I see no harm in using this situation to our advantage. "We'll try one more time. Mr. O'Connor can deliver you to your mother. It will be a good excuse for them to see each other again. All right?"

Georgie grinned at her. "Works for me."

OKAY, so he'd never been known for his tact.

He could have handled it better, Gabe realized. But he'd make up for it tomorrow. Tomorrow would be perfect. He would say and do all the right things. The children would be somewhere else, playing with their new presents or eating cookies or something.

Come to think of it, he wouldn't wait until tomorrow. He would call Maggie now, because the kids were in bed and the presents stacked under the tree and the milk and cookies eaten by Santa. All would be right with the world, and he would talk to Maggie about getting married.

It was the best idea he'd had in a long time. Maybe the best ever—if he didn't count following her home after the party. That ranked right up there in the category of world-class decisions, all right.

The phone rang at the same time he reached for it.

IF THERE WAS any word to use to describe this particular Christmas Eve, Maggie hadn't found it yet.

She'd been frozen with shock when Ella Bliss called after ten o'clock to explain that Georgie was not upstairs in her bed, having sneaked out of the house and ridden her horse to the end of the O'Connors' drive.

Maggie had never heard Georgie leave, probably because she was on her hands and knees cleaning the living room carpet. She'd also been busy scraping burned pizza crust off cookie sheets and maybe even feeling a touch of self-pity.

And now she stood in her living room, watching the distant road and waiting for headlights to turn into the driveway. Gabe was the last person she wanted to see again tonight; her daughter was the first.

Georgie looked anything but apologetic when she entered the kitchen, followed by Gabe. He looked as shaken as Maggie felt, though he did his best not to show it. Here was another good reason Gabe would count himself lucky to stay away from the Moore clan.

"So, you and Joe tried to ride your horses to town." Maggie didn't reach down to hug her daughter. "You both could have been killed."

"Joey said—" Georgie looked at her mother's face and closed her mouth. "I'm sorry. *We're* sorry." She attempted to look past her mother to see if she could see into the living room, but Maggie moved sideways to prevent her from seeing if the presents had been arranged under the tree.

"Where *is* Joey?"

"I took him home first. Along with my mother," Gabe said. "She's good in emergencies."

"Go to bed," Maggie said to her daughter. "And don't make any noise to wake up Lanie. We'll talk about this in the morning."

"Mommy—"

"Go," she said. "Now." Her daughter hurried out of the room, and Maggie didn't speak to Gabe until she heard Georgie's footsteps on the stairs.

"Why—" She faltered. The question was so bizarre. Why did the children go to town on Christmas Eve?

"They wanted to see Ella Bliss," Gabe replied, without her having to ask. He stood tall and handsome by the back door, but he wore his jacket and hat as if he was ready to make a quick getaway.

"Why?"

"Georgie talked to Ella a while ago about finding her a father and, according to Joe, Georgie wasn't real happy with the way things were going."

"At Cal's wedding," Maggie remembered. "It must have started there."

"Before that, I think. You'll have to ask Ella or Louisa, but I guess Georgie made it plain that she wanted me for a stepfather and she wanted help."

"I'm sorry." She couldn't think of a more humiliating situation in which to be. She leaned against the counter and gripped the edge with her fingers. "Don't worry. I'll take care of this."

"Well," the man replied, having the gall to smile. "I could take care of this myself. Right now." In two long strides he was in front of her, his gloved hands on her shoulders. "You could marry me and make everyone—especially me—happy."

"You said you weren't going to propose." She had thought he'd changed his mind. In fact, she was certain of it.

"Not then, not with an audience of tired kids. I thought it should be more romantic. So," Gabe drawled. "Here we are. Alone at last."

"Not exactly."

He looked past her, as if he expected the two little girls to be watching from the living room doorway. Then his gaze fell on her mouth. "What do you mean?"

"I married one man who was in love with Carole Walker and I'm not going to make the mistake of marrying another. So no, getting married is not an option." There. It was out, plain as day. He stared at her as if she had just spoken French.

"Do you want to elaborate on that a little or just leave me in the dark?"

"It wouldn't work."

"Because?"

"I don't want to be second best again," she said, very much afraid she was close to tears. She wanted nothing more than to believe that she could marry this man and love this man and sleep with this man for the rest of her life, but...it was a long shot.

"Second best?" he repeated, removing his hands from her shoulders. "What the hell does *that* mean?"

"You'll never love me the way you loved her. I'm good old Maggie—nothing glamorous or elegant, no college degree or fancy clothes."

"I like your clothes," Gabe muttered. "And I wish I knew what the hell you're talking about." He took off his hat and raked his fingers through his hair before the hat went back on his head. "God knows, Maggie, you've turned second best into a lifestyle."

She crossed her arms in front of her chest. "What is that supposed to mean?"

He waved his arm around the kitchen, taking in the drapes, chairs, table and her oversize chandelier. "Everything else you've got around here has been used before. You don't seem to mind. Cripes, you made a business out of it, didn't you?"

"That's not the same thing."

"Like hell it isn't," Gabe roared, impressing Maggie with his temper. He really thought she would leap at the chance to marry him? Well, she thought, watching him turn and stomp toward the door. She'd leaped at the chance to sleep with him, so she supposed he had a right to get his hopes up.

"Really, Gabe," she tried, calling after him as he twisted the doorknob. "It would never work." *Unless you declare your mad, passionate love for me—which might help. A lot.*

He turned, frowning. "If you expect me to go down on my knees and beg, forget it."

That said, he left. Without slamming the door, too, which might have wakened the girls.

She really did love the man.

MAGGIE DIDN'T SLEEP. Between thinking of all the horrible things that could have happened to two eight-year-olds riding horses to town on a cold dark December night and going over everything said and unsaid between her and Gabe, she couldn't go to bed and drift off to sleep. She'd taken a shower, she'd fixed hot chocolate, she'd been ready for bed and more than a little reluctant to face that cold, wide mattress alone.

So she decided she'd tile a little more of the kitchen backsplash; after all, the tiles and the mastic were sitting in a box under the sink, and the house was quiet. It was after three, and the girls would be up at dawn, which gave her two hours to mope or two hours to accomplish something. So she switched from hot chocolate to hot coffee and went to work.

At sunrise, Gabe walked in without knocking. "Maggie, damn it, this is crazy."

"Not really. We could continue to have sex," she whispered, knowing the girls would be awake soon. He looked gorgeous and frustrated and wonderful, so she poured him a cup of coffee and handed it to him.

"And sleep alone? No way." Gabe set the coffee cup on the table and removed his gloves, shoving them in his pockets, before he approached her.

"That is a problem," she agreed, thinking of her empty bed.

"I love your body." His index finger traced the V of her blue robe, the one he liked so much.

"You hate my furniture." She felt obligated to say that, though she would rather have hauled him up-stairs to her bedroom.

"I can get used to it. The ranch could use sprucing up."

She thought of something else. "I have a business to run."

"So do I."

"I'd like more children," Maggie said, waiting for him to lift his gaze to hers.

"How many?" He looked very, very serious as he untied her robe.

"One. Or two." His hands smoothed the sides of her waist and he urged her body against his.

"No telling what could happen if we slept in the same bed every night," he murmured close to her ear.

"I'd like—" She stopped, feeling as if she was perilously close to bursting into tears. She hated that feeling.

Gabe drew back to look at her. "You'd like what, sweetheart?"

"I'd like," she said, taking a deep breath. "I'd like to know I was loved."

"You are," he said. "I mean, I do. Love you. Very, very much." His fingers gripped her waist as if he was afraid she would move away before he was finished. "I can prove it."

"How?"

"Come on." Before she knew what he was doing, he had taken her hand and led her out the back door onto the porch. "There," he said, obviously very proud of himself. "Your Christmas present."

A gorgeous pale blue pickup truck sat in the driveway. Extended cab, tinted windows, four-wheel drive and a covered bed, all gleamed in the pale sun. The dealer's sticker was still on the driver's window.

"It's *mine*?"

"I bought it Saturday. For you. For Christmas. It's

brand-new," Gabe said. "Not used. Not—what did you call it last night? Secondhand."

"Second best," Maggie said, shivering a little in the cold. Gabe stood behind her and wrapped her inside his open coat.

"Better?"

She was snug against his warmth, all solid muscle and sheepskin. "Yes."

"We both were, you know," he said into her ear.

Maggie turned so she faced him. "Were what?"

"Second best," he repeated, looking at her. "We both were. Carole loved Jeff, Jeff loved Carole, and that left you and me." His arms tightened around her, keeping her warm, keeping her safe. "And now we can be first best, if there's such a thing."

She smiled. "There should be. First best," she repeated. "I like that."

"So you'll marry me, get two kids and a new truck, a new mother-in-law, another ranch house and all—I mean *all*—my love?"

"I didn't know you were so romantic."

"Just answer the damn question, sweetheart."

"I do, I will, of course." And of course she kissed him, met him more than halfway as his mouth descended to claim hers.

"Reach into the left pocket of that jacket," Gabe said, ending the kiss after a long, very satisfactory embrace. Maggie reached out from under the warmth of the jacket and slipped her hand past a glove. Her fingers touched a velvet box.

When she brought it out she held it in the palm of her right hand while Gabe tucked the jacket around her shoulders.

"Open it," he said, and she did. A platinum band, studded with two rows of diamonds, sparkled at her. "It's not from an Idaho brothel, and they're not old rhinestones," he said. "But I know how much you like old jewelry." His smile was wicked, and she knew he was thinking of their night together.

"It's beautiful. And very old. Where on earth did you find it?"

"In the safety deposit box. It belonged to my grandmother."

"And you never—"

"No," he said, knowing exactly what she asked. "I didn't know it existed until my mother produced it a couple of days ago and told me to keep it handy. I think she knew something was going on."

Maggie slipped it on her left ring finger. "I always liked your mother."

"Does it fit?"

"Almost." She could put some tape around the back. She could make it work. She would make a lot of things work.

"I should have fallen in love with you first," Gabe

said, and he kissed the tip of her nose, which she was sure was red.

"But think what a Christmas Eve you would have missed," she told him, tugging him toward the kitchen door.

"I'm thinking," he said, "of Christmas night."

"How, with the kids and our mothers—"

He frowned. "We need to get married. How about tomorrow?"

She stood on tiptoe and kissed his mouth. "I've been waiting since I was twelve for you to say something like that."

Georgie stood in the kitchen watching them enter.

"What's going on? Are you getting married?"

"Yes," Maggie told her. "As a matter of fact, we are."

Her daughter burst into delighted giggles and looked past him to the door. "Where's Joey and Kate?"

"Home," his father said. "And still in bed, I hope. We'll come over later?" The question was directed toward Maggie.

"Yes," she said. "But you'd better go, before they wake up and worry about where you are. You can't miss Christmas."

"I left a note," he explained. "I said I was going to go ask Maggie Moore to marry me and I wasn't coming home until she said yes."

"Kind of sure of yourself, were you?"

Gabe brought her very close to him, to the warmth of his big body.

"I knew you'd give me a second chance," he said.

"Always," Maggie told him, knowing that she'd never been more sure of anything, or anyone, before Gabe. "It's a way of life around here."

Epilogue

THE BRIDE-TO-BE opened her last gift, this one decorated with a spray of silver and white ribbons over silver tissue paper. Inside, in a bed of white tissue, lay an ebony silk nightgown. She held it up to herself and admired the lace that topped the bodice.

"Oh, Ella," she breathed. "How did you know this was exactly what I wanted?"

"You said so, Lou. You wanted black silk." The Hearts Club had decided to meet after Christmas, to surprise Louisa with a wedding shower. "That was when you intended to live in sin," she said rather gleefully.

"It's lovely." Louisa blushed. "Perfect for the honeymoon."

"Did Cameron really propose on Christmas Day?" Missy asked. "That's very romantic."

Lou carefully put the nightgown into its box. "Yes. It was quite a surprise. It turned out that his daughters had a fit when they learned we were going to live together—"

"I wonder why," Ella interjected, her tone wry. That idea had been ridiculous from the get-go.

"And he preferred marriage, too," her sister continued. "So...I said yes, though I am a little nervous. And all of a sudden I'm frightened of such a big step."

"Bridal nerves," Grace said, patting Lou's hand. "You'll be fine."

"But Ella—"

"Ella doesn't mind living alone," Ella declared, knowing it was a lie but something she would adjust to. Father had managed to keep them in this house for over eighty years, which was certainly long enough. Louisa's life as a married woman, with a home of her own, was at least sixty years overdue.

"You have a beau yourself," Lou said. "Maybe Mac will propose, and we could have a double wedding."

Ella gave an inelegant snort. "You must have put too much brandy in your jasmine tea, sister. Mac's a good friend and nothing more." To her chagrin, the other three women burst into gales of laughter.

"Say the word, Ella." Louisa chuckled again. "And the matchmakers will find you a lovely husband."

"No, thank you." She had no idea that the offer would be so terrifying. "I'll manage on my own."

"We had a particularly successful season," Grace said, lifting her coffee cup in a toast. "Owen and Calder are happily married men now, thanks to us."

Missy lifted her cup. "Look at our success with Maggie Moore. I mean, Maggie O'Connor."

"Never mind Maggie," Louisa said. "Georgianna is the one to watch out for. You'd swear that child has some Bliss genes in her from the way she took to matchmaking."

"I'll drink to that," Ella agreed, clinking Mother's delicate china cup against her sister's. "Here's to happily ever after!"

Missie and Grace followed suit, then Missy turned to the others as Ella stood and went to Father's liquor cabinet. "But what on earth are we going to do next year to top this?"

"There is *nothing* that could top this year's matches," Louisa declared. "We've outdone ourselves. Unless—" She gave Ella a searching look, a look that sent chills down Ella's spine and caused her to spill brandy on the sterling serving tray.

"No. I'm quite happy with my life the way it is," she declared.

The others laughed again. Grace took the glass Ella handed her and winked. "That's what everyone says. Until we come along."

"In this town, love has a way of sneaking up on you," Lou said. "Whether you like it or not."

"Here's to Bliss," Ella declared, lifting the small curved glass. Her sister and friends joined her, a gesture that caused Ella to blink back tears. She really was lucky to have such companions, and Louisa was only moving next door, just a few feet away, actually. Surely she would grow accustomed to the change. Ella cleared her throat and added, "And to happily ever after."

A Note from Kristine Rolofson...

I used to have this lovely fantasy about Christmas Eve. The presents are wrapped and under the tree, the children sweetly sleeping in their beds, and my husband and I sit in front of the fire, sip the cognac purchased at a Paris market and exchange our gifts. There is candlelight and soft music and one thing leads to another—I simply must show my appreciation for the antique diamond ring—and, well, you know the rest.

Reality, of course, annihilated my romantic visions every December twenty-fourth. It took a lot of time to put those 127 decals on the Star Wars Millennium Falcon, to piece together a doll stroller, to wrap a guitar so it looked like a lamp. There were six stockings to fill, an egg casserole to prepare for the morning, stuffing to mix, last-minute cookies to frost and a bathroom to clean for the overnight guests called Grandma and Grandpa. By the time we got in bed there wasn't enough time to sleep, never mind do anything else.

"When the children are older," became my mantra. But there was the year I spent Christmas Eve in the emergency room with my youngest son, the time the Christmas gerbils escaped from my closet, the season of the stomach flu. Then small children turned into teenagers who stayed out late and never went to bed. And now that we live in our empty nest, grown children come home and sit late into the night and talk about their new lives—and we are fascinated and grateful, of course, and we do sit in front of the fireplace while we listen.

This Christmas Eve will be similar to the others, my husband will wrap his presents at midnight, when we have run out of gift wrap and all that is left is birthday-printed tissue paper and aluminum foil. I will still fill those stockings; there will be price stickers hanging from my flannel nightgown as I open a bag of store-bought cookies. But maybe this year after everyone has gone to bed, the gifts will be wrapped quickly and we will have a romantic moment or two in front of that fireplace, with the tree lights twinkling and the scents of vanilla and pine filling the room.

Okay, I know it's only a romantic fantasy. But this

year we *will* drink the Paris cognac—if I can remember where I put it.

Merry Christmas to you all.

Best Wishes,

Kristine Rolofson

CALL THE ONES YOU LOVE OVER THE HOLIDAYS!

Save $25 off future book purchases when you buy any four Harlequin® or Silhouette® books in October, November and December 2001,

PLUS

receive a phone card good for 15 minutes of long-distance calls to anyone you want in North America!

WHAT AN INCREDIBLE DEAL!

Just fill out this form and attach 4 proofs of purchase (cash register receipts) from October, November and December 2001 books, and Harlequin Books will send you a coupon booklet worth a total savings of $25 off future purchases of Harlequin® and Silhouette® books, AND a 15-minute phone card to call the ones you love, anywhere in North America.

Please send this form, along with your cash register receipts as proofs of purchase, to:
In the USA: Harlequin Books, P.O. Box 9057, Buffalo, NY 14269-9057
In Canada: Harlequin Books, P.O. Box 622, Fort Erie, Ontario L2A 5X3
Cash register receipts must be dated no later than December 31, 2001.
Limit of 1 coupon booklet and phone card per household.
Please allow 4-6 weeks for delivery.

**I accept your offer! Enclosed are 4 proofs of purchase.
Please send me my coupon booklet
and a 15-minute phone card:**

Name: _____

Address: _____ City: _____

State/Prov.: _____ Zip/Postal Code: _____

Account Number (if available): _____

---

097 KJB DAGL
PHQ401

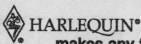